"I am not a$~~$**king $\ldots$ for**
casual sex," Quentin said. "I just want
you to allow yourself to let go. Do you
have to be in control all the time?"

Those were the words Avery remembered from the cab ride from Quentin's loft. Why was it so hard for her to let go? She'd wanted Quentin as much as he wanted her. So why had she run like a scared schoolgirl back to her apartment?

After all, she was a grown woman, wasn't she? She shouldn't have been afraid of taking a risk. Right then and there, Avery vowed that if the opportunity presented itself with Quentin again she would not be so quick to run away. Instead, she would take all he had to offer and then some....

Books by Yahrah St. John

Kimani Romance

Never Say Never
Risky Business of Love
Playing for Keeps

Kimani Arabesque

One Magic Moment
Dare To Love

YAHRAH ST. JOHN

lives in Orlando, but was born in the Windy City—Chicago. A graduate of Hyde Park Career Academy, she earned a bachelor of arts degree in English from Northwestern University. Presently, she is an assistant property manager for a commercial real estate company.

Yahrah first began writing at the age of twelve and since that time she has written more than twenty short stories. When she finally sat down to complete her first full-length novel, she was offered a two-book contract. In 2005, Yahrah was nominated for an Emma Award for Favorite New Author of the Year. Several of her books have received four-star ratings from *Romantic Times BOOKreviews*.

A member of Romance Writers of America, Yahrah is an avid reader of all fiction genres, and enjoys the arts, cooking, travel and adventure sports—but her true passion remains writing.

PLAYING
for KEEPS

YAHRAH ST. JOHN

KIMANI
ROMANCE

KIMANI PRESS™

ISBN-13: 978-0-373-86055-5
ISBN-10:   0-373-86055-2

PLAYING FOR KEEPS

Dear Reader,

I hope you enjoy Quentin and Avery's story. It was a blast to write about commitment-phobic Quentin Davis trying to romance ice-princess Avery Roberts. Quentin's not looking for love—he's just looking for a good time. Until Avery turns his head and he realizes he's not just playing to win a bet—he's playing for keeps.

Quentin's story is the first in the four-book Orphan series. Stay tuned, because Malik's, Sage's and Dante's stories will soon be coming your way.

Please feel free to drop me a note, at yahrah@yahrahstjohn.com, with your thoughts and suggestions. Also be sure to visit my Web site at www.yahrahstjohn.com for the latest contests and book signings in your area.

Best wishes,

Yahrah St. John

Dedication/Acknowledgments

I'd like to dedicate this book to my sister, confidante and best friend Yahudiah Chodosh for all her motivation.

To my father, Austin Mitchell, and my family: the Mitchells, the Smiths, the Bishops and the Astwoods. Thank you for your encouragement and never-ending support.

Last but certainly not least, I'd like to thank all my dear friends—Therolyn Rodgers, Tiffany Harris, Dimitra Astwood, Tonya Mitchell, Diane Alvarez and Phyllis Burton—for keeping me sane and grounded when I think the glass is half-empty. You ladies are the best!

Finally, heartfelt thanks to all the readers who continue to support me as a writer.

Chapter 1

"The lighting is all wrong," Avery Roberts commented to a staff member at the Henri Lawrence Gallery in SoHo, New York City. Located on Houston and Broadway, HLG was an eclectic mix of contemporary art.

"How about here?" Ben tried another position on the wall and glanced in Avery's direction. Everyone knew Avery to be demanding, but Ben had never thought so until now. Slender and strikingly beautiful with café-au-lait-colored skin and green eyes, dressed in a fitted gray pantsuit and pink silk blouse with a V neckline that revealed a hint of cleavage, she was every man's wet dream.

So how could a woman that beautiful be such an ice princess?

Avery smoothed her shoulder-length ponytail and prim bangs with one hand and sighed wearily. "No, no, no." She shook her head. "Move it over there," she ordered, indicating a corner spot in her section of the gallery. It had just the right amount of natural light overhead to reflect her new artist's work.

A buyer at the gallery for several years after attending NYU, Avery knew art. She was well versed in contemporary, Renaissance, baroque and neoclassical art. Ever since she'd been a child, she'd had a fascination with the craft. Thanks in part to her mother, an avid art collector.

"How's it look now?" he asked.

Avery nodded her acceptance. "That's perfect," she replied, walking up to the painting and adjusting it slightly. She was admiring the piece when Hunter Garrett, her boss and the director of the gallery, approached.

"I thought it was fine where it was," Hunter commented from her side.

"No," Avery disagreed. "I think the lighting is better here."

"If you say so."

Why did Hunter always have to be so critical? He always had something negative to say about whatever she did because he thought his skills superior to hers. That was why she didn't care an ounce for Hunter Garrett. Sure, he was tall—he was several inches over her five foot eight—mildly attractive, reasonably intelligent and well dressed. Avery just didn't care for his smug attitude or air of bravado.

Because her father, Clayton Roberts, was vice president of Manhattan Federal Savings Bank and her mother, Veronica Roberts, was queen bee of the socialite arena, Avery had dated plenty of men in her social circle just like Hunter. Arrogant and conceited, men like him thought the sun rose and set on themselves.

"Perhaps you should take a break and join me for lunch," Hunter suggested.

"No, thanks," Avery politely refused. Why would he ask her to lunch when he knew she had tons of work to do before the showing tonight?

"That's too bad," Hunter replied. "I know a great little Japanese place that makes the best sushi."

"I don't eat raw fish," Avery lied, walking away from Hunter and heading toward the stairs that led to their small suite of offices. She loved sushi, but she would never admit it to Hunter. "I like mine cooked, thank you very much."

"Have it your way," Hunter said, from the bottom of the stairs.

"I will, thank you." Avery feigned a polite smile and rushed up to her windowless ten-by-ten office. Once she was safely ensconced within its confines, she fell against the door and breathed a sigh of relief. Somehow she had to get the monkey that was her boss off her back, but how?

"I'm excited to have you back on this side of the Atlantic," talent agent Jason Morgan told his most prized client, photographer Quentin Davis, later that morning at his office on Madison Avenue. "Your work has been on point. And if I do say so myself, it's been some of the best of your career."

"Thank you." Quentin appreciated the compliment, but he was dead tired. He had just flown in on the red-eye from London and had barely had time to drop off his bags and shower at his loft in SoHo before coming to Jason's office. He'd changed out of his favorite pair of Sean John jeans, Skechers and a fitted T-shirt into a more appropriate cashmere cable-knit pullover sweater and trousers for his business meeting.

The problem was he'd stayed a day too long in London for a farewell party thrown by some of his fellow freelancing buddies, and now he was jet-lagged with no one to blame but himself.

"The pictures you took over in Iraq are commanding a high price. Your stay abroad has been very lucrative," Jason commented on Quentin's recent projects.

Quentin smiled. He couldn't complain. He now had a loft in New York and flats in London, Paris and

Rome. Gone were the days of trying to rub two nickels together. His freelancing photography had turned him into a wealthy man and made him one of the most sought after photographers in the business.

The drawback was that as his success as a photojournalist had grown, so had the expectations of the women he'd dated. After several months, many of them wanted a ring on their finger and the security a life as his wife would provide. But he wasn't falling for it. He would not be duped by the gold diggers of the world. His success was his own and one that had been hard to come by after growing up in an orphanage with his best friends Malik Williams, Dante Moore and Sage Anderson.

"That's why we have to stay on top of it," Jason continued. "We have to strike while the iron's hot. Samson Books has approached me about publishing some of your work and *Capitalist Magazine* would like you to do a photo spread on one of the most powerful men in New York. This could be very lucrative for you."

"Sounds great, Jason." Quentin plopped down in the ergonomic leather chair and ran his hands over his bald head. "But I'm exhausted. Five years overseas working nonstop has taken its toll on me. I need a vacation."

Quentin rubbed the sleep from his dark brown eyes. It was way too early for him to be up. He'd forgotten what it was like to be up before noon. He hated the lack of spontaneity of a nine-to-five job. He liked his carefree lifestyle where work was work, but you took time to enjoy life. Americans were too caught up in the rat race. Europeans were much more laid back.

"How long are we talking about?"

Quentin shrugged. "A couple of weeks should do."

Jason sighed. "Oh, thank God. I thought you were about to take a leave of absence, which I would have advised against. You're a hot commodity right now and one of my best clients."

"I'm sure." Quentin smiled. Jason had made a fortune off Quentin's hard work. "All I want to do for the next few weeks is relax."

"All right then. Take a few weeks and call me when you're ready to get back to work."

"Sure thing," Quentin said, rising from his seat. "I'll call you soon." Once he was outside, he took a deep breath and inhaled the spring air. He was on his way to run some errands when his cell phone vibrated in his trouser pocket.

Flipping open the phone, Quentin answered. "Hello?"

"Welcome home, Q!" his friend Sage Anderson shouted from the other end.

Quentin grinned from ear to ear. Sage was his only female friend and he loved her to pieces. She was like his little sister. Perhaps being back in New

York wouldn't be so bad after all. "Sage, it's so good to hear your voice, baby girl."

"You, too," she replied. "How long has it been?"

"Too long."

"Well, I'm dying to see you," she said excitedly, closing the file on the labor case she was reviewing. She was having a devil of a time finding a way out of this mess for her client. "When can we meet?"

"I'm a free agent for a few weeks, so what time would be good for you?"

"How about after work?" Sage suggested. "You know Dante has opened up a tapas bar. We can all meet there."

Quentin rubbed his goatee. "Yes, I had heard, and that sounds fantastic!" And it was about time, Quentin thought. Dante had been a sous-chef for years. He'd cooked for all of them since they'd left the group home at eighteen and Sage at seventeen to live on their own. Tired of the system, they'd been eager to live life on their own terms.

"Say, six o'clock?"

"See you there." Quentin closed the flip phone.

Avery was so busy checking every last-minute detail, from the lighting to music to the caterers, that she didn't notice her best friend, Jenna Chambers, was one of the first guests to arrive.

Jenna was a real stunner with long brown hair cascading down her shoulders, big brown eyes and a curvy figure. Avery was a tad envious at how Jenna always sparkled.

"Avery." Jenna came toward her and gave her a quick hug. "Thanks for the invite."

"No need to thank me. You're doing me a favor. I need all the support I can get," Avery said. She was extremely nervous about Gabriel's first showing. Although Hunter had given her free rein because she'd handpicked their new artist, Gabriel Thomas, she was sure he was hoping tonight would be a bust, which would prove to him that she still had a long way to go when it came to picking new talent.

"And you have it," Jenna said. "Don't sweat. Tonight is going to be just fine. You've been to a million of these things before. And look at you." Jenna grabbed Avery by the hand and twirled her around. "You look classy as always."

Avery was wearing a tapered black Chanel pantsuit and peep-toe Jimmy Choo pumps. "Though I would prefer you to look hot, but that's okay. One of these days, I'm going to get my hands on you and take you down to the Dominic Sabatini Salon for a complete makeover from head to toe." She disliked Avery's bangs and long hair, which was in a perfectly coiffed bun.

Unlike Jenna, who was a talent scout for the Tate Agency where appearance was crucial, Avery didn't need to look sexy. "I need to look competent and knowledgeable so that patrons will come to me for advice, not snag a man."

"That may be true, but you could stand to loosen up a bit, Avery. Sometimes you're too uptight."

"I am not," Avery retorted, folding her arms across her chest. "I just need the show to be a success."

"Is the gallery not doing well?" Jenna inquired, grabbing a crab wonton off the platter the waiter was serving and adding it to the two she was already holding in her napkin. "Hmmm, these hors d'oeuvres are to die for."

"What was that?" Avery hadn't been paying attention. She was watching several buyers peruse Gabriel's oil paintings.

"I asked if the gallery was in trouble."

"Oh no." Avery turned her head and focus back to the conversation at hand. "We're doing fine. There are enough wealthy people in New York to keep us afloat, but you can never be too careful."

"Your mother being one of them," Jenna chuckled.

Avery agreed. "Yes, only the very best for my mother." Veronica Roberts was the crème de la crème of the New York elite and prided herself on supporting the local arts. Her contemporary art collection was one of the finest.

Avery supposed that was why she'd chosen art history as a major at NYU. At a young age she'd been exposed to the finer things in life, from their Park Avenue apartment to the best schools, ballet and piano lessons. Avery was never in doubt that she must excel and be the best at everything she did.

She'd incurred her mother's wrath when she'd adamantly refused her help in obtaining a position at an art gallery. With her mother's connections, Avery could easily have procured a job at a well-known gallery instead of a smaller one like HLG, but Avery was determined to stand on her own two feet without any help from mama bear. And tonight, she would show her mother and Hunter what she was capable of.

"Quentin, it is so good to have you home." Sage squeezed her best friend's shoulders later that evening when they met up after work at Dante's new tapas bar in Greenwich Village, appropriately named Dante's.

Quentin returned the hug with equal fervor. He'd missed Sage. She had come a long way from being a frail eight-year-old girl in need of protection. Now she was a beautiful, poised young woman with smooth brown skin and a lovely shape to boot. The ultra-chic, ultra-short pixie cut suited her round face. And although she was only five foot three, she could be a tigress and extremely protective of the people she loved. He was proud to be considered one of them.

Of course, he'd missed his boys, too. Five years

overseas was a long time to be away from his friends when they were the only family he'd ever known.

"Why did you stay away so long?" Sage punched him in the shoulder. "You know New York is where you belong. Isn't that right?" Sage glanced at their longtime friends Malik and Dante.

They couldn't be more different, Sage thought. Malik was the color of hazelnut, brooding, wore dreads and preferred Afrocentric dashiki, faded jeans and Birkenstock sandals, while Dante, her more level-elheaded friend, was caramel-colored, clean-cut and dressed in preppy khakis and a polo shirt.

"Sage is right. We missed you," Dante said, patting Quentin on the back.

"Well, what can I say?" Quentin shrugged. "I got used to my bohemian way of life abroad. Where time stands still and there's no time limits. No restrictions." Whenever he wanted, he would take long breaks from the hard realities of Iraq and spend some time in one of his flats.

"New York wasn't the same without you." Sage pouted.

"You mean you weren't the same without him," Malik chuckled, swirling around on his bar stool.

Sage turned and glared at Malik. "Same thing. So? How was your first day back in the real world?"

"It was fine. Actually, it was great because I told my agent I was taking a much-needed vacation." Quentin pulled up a bar stool next to Malik.

"I don't believe it," Malik said. "Mr. Workaholic is actually going to take a vacation?"

"How long?" Dante piped in.

"A few weeks."

"Wow, I'm shocked!" Malik said.

Quentin shrugged. "It was time. Plus, I missed you guys."

"Well, I for one couldn't be happier," Sage said beaming. "Now we can get reacquainted."

"Let's drink to your return," Dante suggested and went behind the bar. He pulled out several shot glasses and some Cuervo tequila, their former drink of choice, and set them on the bar. He poured generous shots and pushed them toward the trio.

"To the return of Camelot," Malik said, holding up his shot glass.

"To the return of Camelot," they all cheered, clicked shot glasses and swished the burning liquid down their throats.

Afterward, Quentin turned his shot glass over and said, "What do you say we get out of here? While I was out at a coffee shop earlier, I heard about a new artist's showing tonight at a gallery in SoHo and they always have free food."

"You don't want to eat here?" Dante asked, clutching his heart. "I think I'm offended."

"Of course not, Dante," Quentin replied, leaning over the bar and patting his shoulder. "But I've been out of the art scene too long and need to get my feet wet. There will be plenty of nights spent here, my friend."

"I'm onboard," Sage said. Even though Quentin said he was sticking around, Sage figured she had better spend as much time with him as possible before he bolted out of town for greener pastures.

"Well, I can't," Dante said. "I have to stay here and keep an eye on my investment." His tapas bar had only been open for less than a year, which was make-or-break for a new business, and Dante couldn't afford to fail. He'd put all his savings from years spent as a sous-chef into the restaurant and thus far it was barely making a profit. Several patrons were inside and he had to make sure they had the best tapas experience ever, so they would come back *and* tell their friends.

"I understand completely," Quentin said. "How about you, Malik?"

"Sure, I'll come. Any time I don't have to cook is always a good thing." Malik slipped off the stool. "Dante, pass me my bag." Malik accepted the bag and threw it over his shoulder.

Quentin, Sage and Malik left several minutes later and took the blue line to the Henri Lawrence Gallery in SoHo. They were there within fifteen minutes. They scammed their way past the hostess checking invitations. The gallery was not as trendy as the ones Quentin had frequented in London, but it did have a red carpet, coat check and waiters serving haute appetizers, along with several B-list celebrities, which certainly gave it the appearance of being posh.

Usually on par, Quentin, however, found himself a tad underdressed among this crowd of suit-and-ties and cocktail frocks.

"Quentin, I think we missed the mark on this one," Malik said. His dashiki and Birkenstocks certainly did not fit in. At least Quentin fared better in his pullover sweater and trousers.

Sage sighed. "We're here now. You're just going to have to work it." Sage strutted past several onlookers in her wrap dress and knee-high leather boots to grab three flutes of champagne from the waiter. She returned and handed them each a flute. "See how easy that was?"

"Yes, that was easy for you," Malik said. "Because look at you." He glanced sideways at her. "You look like you just stepped off the pages of a fashion magazine."

Quentin laughed. He admired Sage's confidence and followed her lead by trailing the waiter across the room and taking several hors d'oeuvres off the platter. He popped a few into his mouth.

"Crashing the party, are we?" Avery asked, leaning against a column nearby. She had seen him and his crew of misfits arrive and by the looks of them, it was clear they weren't on her invitation list.

She'd remember if she had invited him. He was tall, dark and handsome. Bald with a sexy goatee and wearing a diamond stud in his ear, he was edgy and certainly not her type, but for some reason she couldn't turn away. The cable pullover sweater he wore did nothing to hide his athletic physique and broad shoulders from her admiring female gaze. In fact, it emphasized that a rock-hard body lay underneath. Avery felt her body heat rising and nervously moistened her dry lips.

Hearing the melodic sound of a feminine voice, Quentin turned around. He wasn't surprised to discover it belonged to a tall, slender beauty with brilliant green eyes. Unfortunately, she was wearing a pantsuit that hid all her God-given assets. *Why did women have to dress up like men?*

"Is it that obvious?" Quentin inquired, placing a hand on the column alongside her face.

Avery stared at his hand. She didn't like the feeling of being closed in by this man, or feeling his warm breath against her face or the smell of his masculine cologne wafting through her nose, so instead she eyed him up and down. "What do you think?" she replied.

Quentin couldn't recall a woman who'd looked at him with such total disdain and it was an instant turnoff. Upon closer inspection, he was able to survey her angular face and scrutinize her slim figure. She was classically beautiful with skin the color of café-au-lait, arresting green eyes and a mass of long hair held in an unflattering bun with bangs, not to mention a narrow waist and petite breasts, which Quentin didn't care for. He preferred his women curvier and with a lot more meat on their bones. Or maybe he was just peeved by the sarcastic tone in her voice?

She pointed to Sage and Malik. "Perhaps you and your friends should think twice about your attire the next time you crash a party, as I'm sure this is not your first." She pushed up from the column, ducked underneath his arm and turned to face him.

"Ouch." Quentin feigned being hurt and touched his chest. "Do you always draw blood at first bite?"

"Only when provoked," Avery returned cattily, folding her arms across her chest as she tried to resist smiling at his clever comeback.

Quentin tried a different approach by explaining himself, something he never did. He didn't know why he was now—perhaps it was the way she scoffed at him? "I'm really not as bad as I appear. I've been in London for a while and flew in this morning on the red-eye. I admit I'm a little tired."

"And in need of a free meal, I presume?" Avery arched an eyebrow.

"So, I take it you think I'm some bum off the street, a freeloader?"

"Aren't you?" she asked, circling around him. And as she did, she received a tantalizing view of his tight rear end. "Here for the free food and drink, that is? I doubt you even know the first thing about art."

"Listen, lady," Quentin began. He didn't appreciate being insulted by a virtual stranger who knew nothing about the hardships he'd endured. He hadn't grown up with a silver spoon in his mouth. "You don't know the first thing about me."

Avery narrowed her eyes. "And I don't care to." She didn't need to. Con artists like him were a dime a dozen in New York. They were always trying to rob good people out of their money.

"Is everything all right over here?" Jenna had returned, carrying several cheese puffs and mini quiches. She glanced back and forth at Avery and batted her eyelashes at the tall, dark and handsome man.

"Everything's just fine," Quentin answered, sipping on his champagne. "It appears your friend thinks I'm a lazy freeloader here only for the free food and drink."

Jenna chuckled. "Hey, so am I." She playfully touched his shoulder with her fingertips. "You should try the mini beef Wellingtons. They are to die for."

"Thanks for the 411." Quentin glared at Avery one final time and walked away.

Avery breathed a sigh of relief once he'd gone. He'd upset her equilibrium when she needed to be calm and cool headed for the evening.

"What was that all about?" Jenna inquired. "I sensed some sexual tension in the air."

"There was nothing sexual between me and that

man," Avery replied haughtily as she watched Quentin underneath hooded eyes.

"If you say so," Jenna said. "But if you ask me, there should have been. You did happen to notice how fine he was."

"I wasn't looking," Avery lied again. She hadn't missed that twinkle in his eyes when he'd spoken or those luscious lips or the way her stomach had curled at the silken sound of his sexy baritone voice.

"Hmmph," was all Jenna could mutter. She didn't buy for one minute that Avery wasn't the least bit attracted.

From across the room, Quentin took the other woman's advice and munched on some mini beef Wellingtons. She was much more his type. Beautiful face, large bosom, curvy bottom and completely feminine, just the way he liked his women.

"So, my boss tells me that I need to log more hours," Sage rattled on. "As if sixty-hour work weeks aren't already enough. Can you believe that?"

"Then, I suggest you chop, chop," Malik said.

As Sage discussed her no-win situation, Quentin stood beside them fuming at the audacity of that ice queen. She hadn't tried to hide her obvious contempt for him and his friends crashing her party.

"What do you think, Q?" Sage inquired, turning sideways.

"What was that?" Quentin asked distractedly.

"I was telling Malik that my job was in jeopardy."

"At least you have one," Malik said.

"What do you mean?" Quentin asked. "I thought you were director of the community center."

"I am but the King Corporation is buying up property on my block all in an effort to build some new entertainment complex and a slew of condos in the neighborhood. If Richard King wins, the Children's Aid Network that owns the property will be forced to sell and I'll be out of a job."

"Didn't he buy up another low-income neighborhood a couple of years ago?" Sage asked. She remembered reading something in the *New York Times*.

"Yes," Malik answered, "which is why I need your help, Quentin." Malik poked him to get his attention since he was staring across the room again at some woman.

"What do you need?"

"Oh, I don't know. You're the photographer. I thought you could come by the center, take a few photos. You know, showcase what a benefit the center is to the community."

"And if these photos were to end up on the front page of a newspaper or some high-profile magazine, then all the better, right?" Quentin asked. Malik wasn't slick. He probably figured with Quentin's connections, a high-profile story might squash the deal.

Malik shrugged matter-of-factly.

"Of course I'll help." Quentin patted Malik's back. "After everything that center did for us, how could I not? If it weren't for Andrew Webster putting a camera in my hand and showing me how to use it, I would not be where I am today. How is the old man anyway?" Andrew had been a wonderful mentor to Quentin.

"Thanks." Malik bumped his shoulder against Quentin's. "Mr. Webster's getting old and has passed the torch to me, but there may not be a legacy for me to continue."

"I understand." Quentin nodded. "Consider it done. Now, if you'll excuse me." He had some pressing business to attend to.

Avery noticed the stranger had joined Nora Stark, a prominent art buyer. She was sure he couldn't hold his own in a conversation with such a heavyweight and was on her way toward him when Hunter stopped her.

"Avery, how are we doing?" Hunter inquired.

"We've sold five paintings thus far."

"That's it? Perhaps you ought to be circulating instead of talking to your girlfriend and that party crasher." So he, too, had noticed they had uninvited guests.

"I could throw them out," Avery suggested. "I thought you might not want any negative press tonight, but if I was wrong, please let me know."

Hunter rolled his eyes. "No, no. I agree with you. Better we allow them a little free food than make a public display."

"Excellent idea," Avery said. "If you'll excuse me." She stalked toward Nora Stark and the stranger, whom she was determined to bring down a peg or two.

"Nora." She kissed either cheek of the older Caucasian woman holding center stage. "How lovely to see you." She had noticed the stranger's eyes narrow when she'd approached.

Nora pulled back and admired Avery's ensemble. "Avery, darling, you're looking splendid as always. How is your mother, dear?"

"Oh, just fine. I'm sure she's eager to get started on that charity auction the two of you are heading." *Take that, mystery man!*

"Quentin, have you met Avery?" Nora asked.

Quentin smiled ruefully. "No, I don't believe I've had the pleasure."

"Allow me to introduce you," Nora said, facing the duo. "Avery Roberts, meet Quentin Davis. I'm sure you've heard of Quentin. He's a world-renowned photographer."

If she could have snapped her fingers and made herself disappear, Avery would have. Quentin Davis. *The Quentin Davis.* She loved his work. His pictures on 9/11 and the war in Iraq were moving. Avery was so embarrassed. How could she have been so far off the mark? She'd totally misjudged him.

When Quentin extended his hand, Avery reluctantly accepted. His fingers were cool and smooth as they grazed hers and Avery's skin felt electrified. What was it about this man that caused the hairs on the back of her arm to stand up at attention?

When Quentin locked gazes with the green-eyed ice princess, she was the first to look away. Was that nervousness he saw in her expression? Surely he couldn't make her uneasy. He doubted that was even possible.

"I think the two of you should talk while I go peruse my next purchase," Nora said over her shoulder as she departed. "I think you have a lot in common."

"Little does she know," Quentin muttered underneath his breath.

"What was that?"

"Oh, nothing," he chuckled to himself.

"So, you…you're a photographer," Avery stuttered. Did she look as dumb as she sounded? "Why didn't you just tell me who you were?"

"Because you were determined to think I was a bum who couldn't afford his next meal. I was leaving you in blissful ignorance."

"Did you just call me ignorant?" Avery asked. *Perhaps you were,* an inner voice said back. Even so, embarrassment quickly turned to annoyance.

"If the shoe fits," Quentin said, shrugging.

"You, you arrogant son of a…"

"Now, now," Quentin leaned down so only Avery could hear him. "I'm sure a lady of your social standing wasn't about to use foul language, were you?"

"You know nothing about my social standing," Avery huffed, taking a step back from Quentin. Why did the softness of his voice whispering in her ear feel like a lover's tender stroke against her skin?

"Oh, please," Quentin replied. "Don't act like that whole kiss-kiss with Mrs. Stark wasn't all about putting me in my place. I may not have grown up wealthy, but I didn't just fall off the turnip truck, either." She was condescending, judgmental and wound as tight as a spring.

Avery's face burned with fury. She couldn't stand that he saw right through her. Or that his nearness was playing havoc with her body. "I'm sorry if I offended you, but you have to admit you did give me a reason to judge you."

"To be a snob?" Quentin queried. "For some reason, I think that comes naturally."

"Well, since I disgust you so much, why don't you stay out of my way for the duration of the evening?"

"Gladly." Quentin stormed away, leaving an upset Avery staring at his retreating form. She wanted to yell at him to get back here so she could be the one to walk away, but he was already back with his friends.

"Who ruffled your feathers?" Sage asked when Quentin returned with a scowl on his face. Malik had abandoned her in favor of hitting on a fellow dreaded woman. "I'll have a cosmo," Sage said to the bartender.

"That ice princess over there." Quentin nodded toward Avery, who was giving him the evil eye.

"You mean the one in the Chanel suit and wearing a fabulous pair of Jimmy Choo shoes?" Sage accepted the drink from the bartender and took a generous sip.

"Yes, the very one."

"Sounds to me like she voiced an opinion that many of the airheads you typically date don't have," Sage commented. "Don't take offense, Q, I just call it as I see it."

"I'm not offended. Because you're right. I like my women docile and pliant," Quentin said. He didn't want some opinionated, repressed, upper-crust broad who wouldn't know passion if it bit her in the butt. He intended to stay as far out of Avery Roberts's path as humanly possible.

Chapter 2

Avery rang the doorbell of her parents' four-bedroom townhome on Park Avenue on Saturday because she'd left her keys at home. Their housekeeper answered.

"Louisa!" Avery exclaimed.

Louisa had been the Roberts family housekeeper for over thirty years. She could have long since retired, but Avery suspected she stayed more for the company than the paycheck.

"Avery, how's my favorite girl?" Louisa enveloped her in a deliciously big hug.

"Oh, I'm just fine. Where's Mom?"

"She's in the kitchen," Louisa replied, taking her

hand. "C'mon in and have a cup of tea and some of my homemade oatmeal-raisin cookies. They are hot out of the oven."

"Oh, that sounds delicious, but I'll only have one." Although she could indulge in what she wanted and never gain a pound, Avery tried to eat right.

She found her mother seated in the large kitchen drinking a cup of Earl Grey tea. Casually dressed in Ralph Lauren capris and a tank top, with her hair in a loose chignon, her mother looked as if she were off for a day in The Hamptons as opposed to an afternoon of spring cleaning. Her mother was determined to rid her attic of clutter. Unwanted art would go to her favorite museum and several local galleries.

"Mom." Avery leaned down, gave her mother a gentle squeeze and took the seat opposite her. Her mother looked beautiful as always, even without makeup. The only way you could tell her age was by the few fine lines around her eyes.

"Have a cup of tea," her mother ordered.

Avery did as she suggested and on cue, Louisa appeared with a teakettle and a packet of English Breakfast tea, Avery's favorite. She let it steep for several minutes before adding milk and sugar. "Where's Dad?"

"Oh, he's playing racquetball at the club with one of his buddies," her mother replied, "and it's for the best anyway, because he'd be trying to keep junk instead of throwing it out."

Her mother was right. Her father was something of a pack rat. "I spoke with Nora and she told me you did quite well at your showing."

Did her mother have spies? "Yes, we sold eight paintings of Gabriel's work," Avery said. "I'm really pleased with the outcome because he was my find, you know."

"That's wonderful, dear," her mother said, even though Avery knew what she wasn't saying. And that was, had Avery invited her, she would have done a lot better. Veronica would have been sure to invite all her friends, and Gabriel's show would have sold out. "And to show my support, I purchased two as well."

"Mom, you didn't have to do that." Avery was annoyed that her mother had to meddle. She just couldn't stay out of her affairs.

"What's the harm? I am your mother after all and I only want what's best for you."

"Yes, but you know I wanted to do this on my own."

"You don't have to be *alone,* Avery. I have connections. This could all have run much smoother if you'd just let me help. Why must you be so stubborn?" her mother said exasperatedly. "You shouldn't even have to work."

"Mother, you know I enjoy what I do."

"True, but you are too ambitious for your own good. If you just found yourself a nice husband and settled down, life would be much easier."

"I don't want to *settle down* and I most definitely don't need you questioning my judgment, Mother. I get enough of that at work," Avery replied.

"And who's doing that?"

"Hunter Garrett."

"Oh," her mother chuckled. "I've dealt with him before. He's a pussycat. Don't worry about him."

"There you go again, dismissing my feelings as if they don't count. I don't know why I even bother," Avery said, rising from the table and grabbing her purse.

"Where are you going?"

"Someplace where I can feel appreciated," Avery returned, walking out of the kitchen. She was tired of her mother's constant criticism that she was too ambitious and too driven. She was quite capable of looking after herself. Avery didn't need to marry some rich guy and be his showpiece. "Tell Daddy I said hello," Avery said over her shoulder as she left.

"Why haven't you returned any of my calls?" Jenna asked when she met up with Avery on Friday evening for dinner. They were standing in the foyer of a new restaurant waiting for a table.

"I'm sorry," Avery apologized and hung her head low. "It's been a tough week."

"No kidding." Jenna grabbed Avery by the chin and peered into her face. There were lines around her eyes. "Have you gotten enough sleep? You look haggard, my dear."

"Thanks a lot," Avery said, snatching her head away.

"Is everything okay?" Jenna asked. "I can tell something's wrong. You aren't yourself. What's going on?"

The hostess interrupted them before she could answer and led them to a table that had suddenly become available.

Avery wasted no time spilling her guts once they were seated. "Oh, the usual. A fight with my mother."

"That seems to be par for the course these days."

"Jenna, sometimes she and I are like oil and water. We just don't mix. You think she'd be proud that I'm doing so well at the gallery, but she's always quick to point out my shortcomings. Or my single status. A girl of your age," Avery mimicked her mother's voice, "should already be married and settled by now."

"She didn't try and set you up again, did she?" Veronica Roberts was notorious for setting Avery up on unsuccessful blind dates, much to Avery's chagrin.

"No, but she would have tried if I'd given her the opportunity."

"Well, forget about her for tonight and let's have some fun. How about some jazz later?"

"That sounds like a fabulous idea." Avery could use the distraction.

After dinner, Avery and Jenna found themselves

at Blue Note. Known for its late-night grooves and full house, Avery wasn't sure they'd get in, but one of Jenna's former models just so happened to be the bouncer at the door and squeezed them in. As they walked to the bar, Avery spied someone familiar seated at a table with some friends. As she approached, Avery realized it was none other than Quentin Davis, the photographer she'd made a fool out of herself in front of last week.

"Cover me," Avery said, pushing Jenna in front of her.

"Why?" Jenna asked over her shoulder.

Avery didn't answer until they were safely past his table and seated in a corner at the bar. "You remember that guy from my showing last week?"

"You mean the good-looking one you were rude to?" Jenna asked. "Then yes, I remember him."

"Well, he's over there." Avery motioned with her head toward the front of the room. When Jenna went to turn around, Avery stopped her. "Don't look. You'll draw attention to us. Let's just stay over here and hopefully they'll leave soon."

"You hope."

"Yes, I do," Avery replied. The last thing she needed was another round with Quentin Davis.

Across the room, Quentin, Sage, Malik and Dante were having a good time laughing and reminiscing about the good ol' days.

"Do you remember when Mr. Peeples caught us sneaking back in after curfew?" Dante asked.

"Oh yeah, we had just turned sixteen, gotten a fake ID and decided we were grown enough to go out on our own," Malik continued.

"That's until we got jumped by those older guys, had all our money stolen and ended up walking twenty blocks home in the rain," Quentin remembered.

"And then Mr. Peeples caught us and put us on dish detail for a month," Dante finished.

"Yeah, those were the days," Malik said.

Sage's brow furrowed. "Why don't I remember that story? Where was I?"

"That's because you were only fifteen, kiddo, and we had to leave you at home," Quentin teased as he rose to his feet. "And you did nothing but sulk for days that you had been left out of all the excitement."

"I did not," Sage returned, even though she recalled being somewhat of a brat afterward.

"You did, too," Quentin whispered in her ear as he leaned down. Once he made it to the bar, he ordered a bucket of Miller Lite and was glancing around the room when his eyes rested on a female frame at the corner of the bar. It was that ice queen from the gallery who'd treated him as if he'd crawled out of the gutter.

Great, Quentin thought. All of a sudden the air in

the bar turned chilly. The bartender slid him a bucket and Quentin slipped him a twenty. "Keep the change."

Quentin sat back into his seat with a frown. "Guess who's here?" he asked, grabbing a bottle out of the bucket.

"Who?" Sage asked, looking around.

"Remember that woman from the gallery?"

"The one in the Chanel suit who was pissed we crashed her showing?"

"The one and only."

"Why don't you go over and say hello?" Sage suggested. "You know, get off on a better foot?" Sage knew the woman had gotten to Quentin.

"I don't think so," Quentin said. "That woman's as cold as ice."

"Remember when we used to make bets with each other to go out with someone and see how long we'd last?" Malik asked. "Well, I'll bet you twenty bucks—" he pulled out his wallet and slid a twenty Quentin's way "—that you can't melt that ice queen."

"You're joking," Quentin said, pushing the money back toward Malik. "We haven't done that since we were teenagers."

"Who said we ever have to grow up?" Dante replied. "Do it. And for added incentive, let's up it to fifty." He slid another thirty dollars across the table.

Quentin considered it for a moment. They thought

he couldn't melt the ice around that diva's heart. Sure, it would be difficult, but he was Quentin Davis after all. "All right, you're on." He accepted the bet, tucked the bills in his pocket, grabbed his bottle of beer and stood up ready to face off against the dragon lady.

"Wait!" Sage yelled when Quentin started to walk away. She jumped up from her chair and tucked another fifty bucks in his pocket. "Don't leave me out." She kissed Quentin on the cheek, smacked him on the butt and said, "Go get her, tiger, urgh."

Quentin strutted to the back of the room and walked up to Avery Roberts, who was sitting at the bar with her back to him. She was with that sexy friend of hers from the showing. Quentin would have preferred the bet was on her as it would be much more enjoyable, but alas it wasn't. Quentin coughed. When Avery didn't turn around, he coughed again.

Avery swiveled around in her bar stool and was surprised to find Quentin standing behind her. "What do you want?" she asked a little too sharply.

Although Quentin didn't care for her tone, he persevered. He was always up for a challenge. He smiled and said, "Ladies." He nodded over to her friend.

"Hi, how are you?" Jenna smiled back flirtatiously.

"Oh, I'm fine," Quentin replied. "I'm just here with some friends listening to the jazz band. They're great, aren't they?" He placed his beer bottle on the bar and moved closer to Avery.

"Yes," Avery said curtly. She didn't like that he was so close to her. It unsettled her. "Now, can I help you with something?" She ignored Jenna, who was glaring at her.

Quentin took a deep breath and willed himself to calm down before responding. "Well, I came over to apologize for last week." At Avery's blank stare, he continued. "You know, crashing your showing. My friends and I really shouldn't have come without an invitation. I hope we didn't cause you any trouble."

Avery was shocked when Quentin apologized. She hadn't seen that one coming. Now she felt two feet small because once again, she'd misjudged him. But this time instead of insulting him, she'd be the bigger person. Especially since being angry took too much energy and after arguing with her mother she was fresh out. "No apologies necessary. No harm, no foul."

"Great." Quentin smiled. And when he did, Avery's heart skipped a beat. Why was it she hadn't noticed what a great smile he had? Could it be because she'd been too busy judging him? Perhaps he'd been right last week when he'd implied she was judgmental. She would have to work on that. "So, how about I buy you ladies a drink?"

Her initial reaction was to say no, but then Avery thought better of it. "Thank you, I'd like that," she replied.

"Bartender, I'll have two…" He glanced over at their empty glasses.

"Apple martinis," Avery offered.

"Two apple martinis, please," Quentin said. When the barkeep returned with two glasses, Quentin handed each of the women one and raised his bottle. "To new beginnings."

"To new beginnings," Avery and Jenna chimed in and clinked glasses before sipping their martinis. From her perched view atop the bar stool, Avery was nearly face to face with Quentin, and what a face it was. She allowed herself to enjoy the view. Smooth, sexy chocolate skin, broad nose, full lips and a glistening bald head made Quentin Davis one very attractive man. He was wearing a royal-blue silk shirt, tucked into black trousers along with two pieces of jewelry, the diamond stud she'd seen before in his ear and a St. Christopher cross that dangled from his neck.

The band struck up a slow ballad and couples began filling the small dance floor. Quentin realized that a slow dance was a prime opportunity to make his move and put all the Davis charm on Ms. Roberts.

"Would you like to dance?" Quentin asked. He chugged the rest of his beer and placed the empty bottle on the bar.

Avery shook her head. "I really don't dance. I'm terrible at it. I have absolutely no rhythm."

Quentin chuckled. "You can't be that bad." He took the martini glass out of her hand and pulled Avery to her feet.

"No," Avery resisted. "I'm really that bad. Why don't you take Jenna?" Avery glanced in her friend's direction, but Jenna shook her head.

"He didn't ask me," Jenna said. "And I'm not finished with my drink anyway." She held up her full martini glass.

"There, it's settled." Quentin placed his hand on the small of Avery's back and led her to the dance floor, much to her dismay.

"I warn you, I'm very bad," Avery said.

"Don't worry, I'll lead." Quentin encircled her waist with his arm and pulled her toward him. Thanks to the crowded dance floor, they were thigh-to-thigh and cheek-to-cheek. When Avery squirmed and tried to put some distance between them, Quentin pulled her even closer until her small pert breasts were resting firmly against his chest. Slowly and deliberately, he moved her slender body with his to the rhythm of the music.

Being so close to Avery allowed Quentin an opportunity to see what he'd really gotten himself into with this bet. She smelled fantastic. Soft, light and airy—fresh and ripe for the picking. His second thought was that she was much prettier than he'd originally thought, especially if she did a little bit more with her hair rather than having it pinned up all the time. Quentin wished he could take out every pin and run his fingers through her long hair and make it unruly. Avery Roberts needed to be cut loose from her restraints.

As Quentin glided her across the dance floor, with one big strong hand clasped firmly in hers, Avery wasn't surprised to find that he was a skillful dancer. He looked like the sort who knew how to move a woman's body. She tried not to peer into his arresting dark eyes for fear she'd get lost in them and step on his feet. She needn't have worried; Quentin kept her on the floor through several slow tunes and didn't release his hold on her until the tempo changed.

"See, you're not as bad as you think," Quentin whispered in her ear once the dance was over.

"That's because you were guiding me," Avery said. "Anyway, thanks for the dance."

"You're welcome. Maybe we can do it again sometime?"

"Maybe."

Quentin joined her back at the bar but not before glancing at his friends, who were giving him an enthusiastic thumbs-up. Quentin smiled. His friends knew him well enough to know that Avery would be putty in his hands in no time. Quentin wasn't arrogant about his prowess. He had a way with women and he had an oversize black book to prove it, with names from across the Atlantic.

"Aren't you going to rejoin your friends?" Avery asked. "You don't have to stay and keep us company."

"Perhaps I find your company more appealing," Quentin said silkily.

"I, uh…" Avery couldn't think of a proper comeback. Why did he have to say things like that? Was he trying to throw her off-kilter?

"Well, I'm exhausted." Jenna faked a yawn and stretched her arms. "I think I'm going to head out." She stood up, reached for her clutch purse and plopped her credit card on the bar. "Since you've had a rough week, drinks are on me tonight."

"Jenna." Avery turned and pleaded with her eyes for her best friend to stay, but Jenna ignored her and settled the bill with the bartender. When she was done, she leaned over and whispered in her ear, "Relax and enjoy." She gave Quentin a wave before exiting.

"What did Jenna mean you had a rough week?" Quentin inquired.

"I had a disagreement with my mother."

"I'm sorry to hear that," Quentin said, taking the stool vacated by Jenna. "Perhaps I can remedy that."

"Not so fast, Mr. Quentin Davis." Avery placed a hand on his chest to stop him. And when she did, she wished she hadn't. Quentin's chest was broad and rock hard. "Just because we shared a dance does not mean anything is going to happen here."

"Must you always be so combative?" Quentin asked, sitting down. "A drink and a few laughs amongst friends might cure your bad mood."

"So we're suddenly bosom buddies now? You don't even like me very much."

"I thought we were off to a brand-new start, but if I was wrong…" He rose to his feet.

When he did, Avery realized she didn't want him to go. "No, no, you weren't wrong. Sit back down."

That was when Quentin knew he had her.

"I'm sorry," Avery apologized and shook her head. "Listen. It's not you. It's me. I'm going through a rough patch right now and although I appreciate the drink, I'm really tired and going to head home."

"Sure I can't tempt you to have another drink?" Quentin asked. He'd seen the anguish in her eyes.

"Not tonight." Avery stood up, turned on her heel and walked out the door, leaving a frustrated Quentin in her wake.

His charm usually worked on most women, but apparently not on Avery Roberts. It had only worked as much as she'd allowed it to work. For a moment he'd been sure he'd gotten to her, but just as quickly the moment had passed. He was going to have to work a lot harder to break the ice around Avery.

He returned to the table where his friends sat with gigantic smirks on their faces. "What's wrong, playa? Did she shut you down?" Malik joked.

"Seems someone has bitten off more than he could chew," Dante chuckled.

"Oh, leave him be," Sage said.

Trust his little sis to always defend him, Quentin thought.

"Forget them." Sage turned to Quentin. "You said she was a cold fish."

Quentin shook his head. "It wasn't that. There was something else."

"An aversion to playas," Malik suggested.

Quentin laughed from deep within his belly. "No. Something was troubling her. I could see it in her eyes."

"Then, you're just in time to help a damsel in distress," Dante said. "It's Quentin to the rescue."

"If I didn't love you so much, I'd have to hurt you." Quentin laughed.

"So, what's next?" Sage asked.

"I don't know." He rubbed his goatee. "I'm going to think about it. Because, trust me, the next time I meet Avery Roberts, she will not walk away."

"Those are some big words, my man," Malik said. "Now let's see if you can back them up."

"Oh, he can back them up," Sage continued.

"You better believe I can," Quentin boasted.

Chapter 3

The following Monday, Quentin stopped by the old neighborhood in Harlem to visit the community center that he, Malik, Dante and Sage had frequented as children. The center had been an oasis for them after having been seen as a bunch of misfits at the orphanage: the troublemaker, the angry boy, the nerd and the sickly girl. Since he had so much free time now that he was on vacation, he could finally make a difference and volunteer. Perhaps he could be a positive influence in a child's life.

After exiting the blue train, Quentin was surprised at how much the area had stayed the same. Sure, there were some pockets that even he wouldn't be caught dead in in the middle of the night, but all in all, not much had changed. It was sure a far cry from his current digs in SoHo. Quentin smiled to himself as he opened the center's tattered front door. He'd come a long way, although the same could not be said for the door.

He gave his name to the receptionist at the front counter and signed in on the guest list. She wasn't Vivienne Falconer, the old battle-ax who used to give him, Malik and Dante a hard time, but she sure looked as if she could check a young brother if needed and scare him into acting right. She waved for him to come back.

Malik came rushing out a side office just as Quentin came through the door separating the lobby from the offices. "Wow, I'm surprised you came."

Quentin tried not to take offense at his best friend's comment. "You did ask me to come by and take some photographs, or did I miss a beat somewhere?"

"No, of course not," Malik replied. "I'm sorry, Quentin. It's been a trying morning. Come on in." He brought him into his small office.

As Quentin looked around, he saw that it too was in need of a paint job. He determined right then and there to give a generous donation to fix up the community center, that was if he had the opportunity to do so and the corporation Malik had mentioned didn't take over the neighborhood.

"It's all right," Quentin laughed and settled back into a chair across from Malik's desk. "If I didn't love you like a brother, I might be offended. But since I do, I'll let it slide."

"I am really grateful you came, Q," Malik said. "The King Corporation has been targeting several store owners on this block and offering them big checks to sign over their property, and now the community center has been approached."

"What are you going to do?"

"Children's Aid Network sponsors the center and as the director, I have no intention of selling to the King Corporation so that fat cats like Richard King can get richer and richer while the poor in this community are displaced."

"What can I do to help?"

"I need you to use all your connections and put a big spotlight on this, so that the community and beyond are aware of what's happening." Malik stood up as he gave his impassioned speech. "The people in this community are looking to the center and C.A.N. to help, to stop this travesty from happening. They don't want to sell. Many of these store owners have owned their property for years, before the King Corporation had any interest in *re-developing* it."

"I know a lot of big names that would eat a story like this up," Quentin said. He could see it spread across the *New York Times* or *Post*: Big Corporation

Versus Low-Income Community. "I'll call up a few contacts. Otherwise, I am at your disposal."

"It's been a while since you've been back," Malik said. "Why don't you walk around, get a feel for the place and take some of those candid photographs that capture a nation. In the meantime, I have some paperwork to finish up here."

"Sure thing." Quentin stood up and threw his camera bag over his shoulder. He didn't need Malik to give him a tour of the community center because it had been his second home in his youth.

The center housed computer and game rooms, a basketball court, dance room, swimming pool and not to mention a clinic. The neighborhood relied on the free health care and dentistry the center provided along with the Head Start and after-school programs. He stopped by each in hopes of using his camera as a tool to show the unseen or the forgotten. He got some great shots of the dancers with their graceful movements, but his favorite was of the toddlers because it captured the wide-eyed innocence of youth. As he strolled down the halls, Quentin realized just how much responsibility Malik had on his shoulders.

His final stop was the gymnasium where several male teenagers were shooting hoops. Quentin quietly came in and stood along the sidelines. As he snapped photos, one of the young men looked over at him and then nudged his friends. "Hey! What you doing with that camera?"

"Just taking a few pictures," Quentin replied, looking up from the lens. "I hope you don't mind."

"That depends on what you're going to do with them." His friends snickered behind him.

"Well…" Quentin rubbed his goatee. "They might end up in a newspaper or magazine or perhaps on television."

"Why? Are you famous?" the young man inquired. "'Cause I sure don't know you."

"In a way, yes—I'm a photojournalist."

"What's that?" another boy asked.

Quentin shook his head. It was a shame that these young men had no idea of what he did for a living because they were not exposed to anything outside their daily lives. Quentin resolved to do all he could to stop this corporate giant from railroading another low-income community.

"I take pictures and sell them to magazines and television stations and they publish them or put them on the air."

"Wow, that's kinda cool," the first young man said. "How's the Benjamins on something like that?"

A laugh echoed from deep within Quentin's belly. "The Benjamins are quite good. But you have to work hard and learn your craft before you really start to get paid. Have any of you guys ever taken a photography class here at the center?"

"Photography?" The young man's voice rose. "Naw, man, we 'bout playing ball."

"Life isn't all about basketball and having fun. You should try something new sometime and if you're interested," Quentin continued, "I might be persuaded to come and teach you the basics of photography."

"You would?" The boys sounded shocked that he would go out of his way to help them.

"Yes, I would," Quentin replied honestly, just as Mr. Webster had helped him and showed him how to work a camera.

"That sounds like an excellent idea," a masculine voice said from behind him. Quentin turned around and found Malik grinning from ear to ear. "You boys are in severe need of a hobby."

Malik walked toward them. "That's a really generous offer, Quentin." He took Quentin aside. "And I understand if you didn't mean it. I know how busy you are. If you want to just take the pictures, that's fine with me."

Quentin shook his head and patted Malik's shoulder. "It's no imposition. I could stand to give back a whole lot more."

Malik chuckled. "See?" He pointed a knowing finger at Quentin. "You have to work. You can't just relax."

"I've been doing nothing but taking it easy for a week now. And if I can open up some young men's eyes to the joy of photography, then all the better." He turned back around to the young men. "I'll be back the week after next, after I get a few supplies and we can get started. And you," he said to Malik, "I'll see later."

Malik mouthed the words *thank you* as Quentin headed out the swinging doors.

"Daddy, it's so good to hear from you," Avery said when he telephoned her later that week. "What's going on?"

"I was hoping you would make up with your mother," Clayton Roberts said from the other end of the line. "She's been walking around sullen all week and still wants your help cleaning out the attic."

"Daddy…"

"You know how your mother can get," her father said.

"You mean critical and controlling?" Avery asked bitterly.

"No, I mean overprotective. You know she only wants what's best for you."

Why did her father always take her mother's side?

"She has a funny way of showing it." Avery huffed. If she didn't have anything nice to say, then maybe she shouldn't say anything at all—but Avery didn't dare say that to her father.

"Have you ever thought that maybe you're being overly sensitive?"

Avery paused. Perhaps he had a point. Her mother did have a way of getting to her, and Avery let her. "All right, I will make amends, but only for you."

She was a daddy's girl after all. He always seemed to understand her more than her mother. He never criticized. Instead, whenever she had a problem, he offered a shoulder or an ear and just listened. Unlike her mother, he never tried to control the outcome.

"Good, sweetheart. I'll see you on Saturday then?"

"Sure, Daddy."

Avery arrived on Saturday as promised and found the attic in complete disarray. Her mother had already gotten started and there were tons of boxes, trunks, paintings and various sculptures and artifacts from her mother and father's travels during the years, and from the looks of it, her parents hadn't gone through anything since she was a child, which made it over thirty years' worth of junk.

"I'm glad to see you could make it," her mother said coolly as Avery rolled up her sleeves and donned a scarf to protect her hair from the dust and spiders.

Avery ignored the dig. She was sure her mother thought she had completely overreacted last week. "Why don't we tag everything you do want," Avery suggested, "and we'll throw away what you don't want."

"Sounds good to me," her mother said.

Two hours later, they had made progress and had managed to clear a path out to the hallway, but only because Louisa had assisted after finishing her chores.

"I don't know about you guys, but I'm ready for lunch," Louisa spoke up.

"Lunch would be great, Louisa. Can you whip us up some sandwiches?" her mother asked.

"Already done. I premade the sandwiches, and the soup just needs to be heated up," Louisa replied. "I'll go warm it up now."

While they waited, Avery and her mother continued cleaning until Avery stumbled upon a chest that had been hidden by some old carpeting. That was when all hell broke loose.

"I wonder what's inside," Avery said.

No sooner were the words out of her mouth than her mother yelled, "Don't open that trunk!"

"Why? It's just an old trunk," Avery replied. She was opening the lid when her mother nearly leaped across the room and shut it. And to make matters worse, she sat on the lid.

"Mother! What's gotten into you?" Avery looked up questioningly at her mother, who looked as white as a ghost. She didn't understand what the big deal was. "Is there something in that chest I'm not supposed to see?"

"Of course not," her mother laughed nervously.

"Then why won't you move?" Avery asked.

"If you must know," her mother said, "there are some old love letters from your father in that trunk and I'd like them to remain private."

"Is that all?" Avery smiled. "Why didn't you just say so?" She rose to her feet.

Her mother didn't have time to answer because Louisa called up to them that Clayton had returned from racquetball.

"C'mon, let's go eat." Her mother headed down the stairs, but Avery held back.

Her mother's reaction to that trunk disturbed her. The knowledge that she could be hiding something caused her to rush over to it. Should she open Pandora's box? Maybe what was inside was best left hidden.

Despite her reservations, Avery opened the lid. Inside were some newborn baby clothes and a swaddling blanket. Was this what she'd been brought home in? Avery's eyes misted with tears. Why hadn't her mother ever shown her these before? She continued her fact-finding mission and dug through the trunk until she found a leather portfolio.

Curious, Avery popped open the lock and looked inside. The contents appeared to be important legal documents. Avery was quickly scanning them for a clue of what her mother could be hiding when she saw the word *Adoption* in big letters across the front page of one of the papers. Avery was in shock as she continued to read the document that stated in plain English, that Mr. and Mrs. Clayton Roberts had adopted an infant baby girl born on November 3, 1974.

"Ohmigod!" Avery fell back in horror and tears streamed down her face. "No, no, this can't be. This can't be." She shook her head. She was adopted! Her parents weren't really her parents?

A million questions went through Avery's mind as understanding dawned on her. Holding the paper in her hand, she realized that this was why her mother didn't want her to open that trunk. She didn't want the truth to come out, which was that they'd been lying to her from the day she was born. What Avery didn't understand was why hadn't they told her? It wasn't as if she wasn't old enough to learn the truth. Why had they kept this from her? And if she wasn't Avery Roberts, who was she? Who were her real parents?

Avery wept aloud, rocking back and forth, and didn't hear the attic floor creak or see her parents walk in.

"Oh, Avery." Her mother fell to the floor and pulled a distraught Avery into her arms. "Oh, baby, I'm so sorry…." Her mother cried, holding Avery close to her heart.

"So, it's true, then?" Avery asked as she held on to her mother for dear life. "I'm adopted?"

Silence ensued, fracturing whatever thread of hope Avery had had that the document wasn't real.

Her mother nodded. "Yes, but we never wanted you to find out this way. We wanted to tell you."

"Why didn't you?" Avery choked out. "Why didn't you tell me?"

Her father kneeled down beside her. "I don't know, baby girl. I suppose we were just selfish and wanted you all to ourselves. Ever since the day you were born, you've been the light of our lives."

"My whole life has been a lie."

"That's not true." Her mother shook her head.

Avery flung herself out of her mother's arms. Her father tried to help her from the floor, but Avery refused his help and rose on her own. "How can you say that? Everything has changed. I don't even know who I am."

"You are our daughter, Avery Roberts." Her mother's voice rose vehemently. "Nothing has changed."

"How can you say that?" Avery asked, nearly hysterical. "Everything has changed! You lied to me. You should have told me long ago that I was adopted. My God, I've always wondered why people said I looked nothing like the two of you. Why I always felt out of place, like a square peg in a round hole."

When her parents stared at one another without answering, Avery yelled at them. "Where does a black girl with green eyes who looks almost white come from? Where do I come from?"

Avery was upset because her father was doing his stoic routine while her mother hung her head low and remained silent. "Where do I come from? Answer me!" A hot tear trickled down her cheek.

"What do you want to know?" her father asked.

"I want to know about my biological mother," Avery said, folding her arms across her chest.

"Your birth mother was very young and she wasn't ready to be a parent," her father replied.

Avery nodded and wiped a tear from her cheek

Yahrah St. John 59

with the back of her hand. "That explains her reasons for giving me up. What were yours for adopting?"

When her mother finally spoke she stammered. "I'll—I'll answer that." She rose to her feet. "Your father and I wanted a newborn. We were evaluated and screened like any other adoptive parents."

"That doesn't answer my question," Avery said.

"Avery, does it really matter?" her father asked. He knew this was a touchy subject with Veronica and he didn't want his wife or his daughter to suffer anymore.

"Yes, it does," Avery said adamantly.

Her mother walked over to the small window overlooking the tree-lined street and stared listlessly out of it. Neither of her parents spoke for several long, excruciating minutes.

When her mother turned around, her cheeks were stained with tears. It hurt Avery to see her mother in pain, but she would not be dissuaded. She wanted the whole truth and nothing but. She deserved that much.

"We adopted you because I couldn't have any children," her mother said. "I couldn't give your father a child and despite my shortcomings, he stayed with me. He vowed we'd have a family someday and we did. We had you."

"Oh, Veronica." Her father came toward her mother and pulled her into his arms. She collapsed under the emotional strain, but he didn't let go, he just held on tighter.

Avery did feel a pang of guilt. It couldn't be easy for her mother to admit that she wasn't perfect, that she was flawed like the rest of the human race. "I know this is difficult for you, but imagine what this is like for me," Avery said. "I need answers."

"Honey, now is not the right time," her father said over his shoulder. "Can't you see your mother is upset?"

Turning blindly, Avery dropped the adoption papers and stumbled down the stairs. She couldn't stand it anymore. Knowing that her parents, the people she'd confided in, loved and trusted the most, had betrayed her was beyond unbearable.

Seeing Avery upset, Louisa instinctively called out to her, but Avery shook her head, grabbed her jacket off the coatrack and rushed out the door.

Somehow she managed to hail a cab and once inside she fell against the back seat. Her whole world was falling apart. Avery covered her mouth with her hand and smothered the grief that threatened to spill out. How could this be happening?

A short while later as she rode the elevator up to her apartment on Central Park West, the future looked bleak. Her mind was spinning and she had no idea how she was supposed to go on after learning her life was built on a lie. Once she was inside her apartment, she felt sick to her stomach and barely made it to the bathroom before purging her breakfast. Afterward, she fell down to the floor and let out a gut-wrenching sob.

* * *

Avery's emotions raged over the weekend as she reeled from the knowledge that she'd been adopted. She tried losing her sorrows on the piano by playing sad music, and when that didn't work she did the one thing that usually made her feel better and that was making pottery. Once she felt the moist lumps of clay in her hands as she sat over the potter's wheel, with her foot on the treadle, Avery felt somewhat calm. But then, out of nowhere she had a bout of hysteria that had her so debilitated she had to leave the wheel. Hours later, she'd accomplished nothing. Somehow she managed to put one foot in front of the other and make it to work on Monday. She masked her inner turmoil to her coworkers and boss even though she was dying inside.

The only thing she was sure of after she'd cried her eyes out was that she had to find her biological mother. Even if the woman didn't want to have anything to do with her, she had to find out where she came from, or at least that was what she told herself. But Avery secretly hoped that her biological mother would want to have a relationship with her. She knew that it would hurt her parents to hear she was launching a search, but this was something she had to. If she didn't, she would always wonder and never be free.

The problem was that when she called the New York State Department of Health to obtain an original copy of her birth certificate, she discovered that all adoption records were sealed. They suggested she register with reunion agencies or petition the court to open her adoption file. All of which could take a considerable amount of time and Avery had to have answers now. What she needed was to find an honest, reliable private investigator to research her past. Luckily, one of her sorors, Julia Peoples, a fellow alpha kappa alpha from NYU, was a criminal attorney. Avery was sure Julia used investigators in her line of work and if she didn't, she might know where to look.

After picking up the phone, Avery nervously dialed Julia's number; thankfully she picked up on the second ring. "Julia, how are you, darling? It's Avery."

"Avery, long time no hear," Julia said. "How are you?"

"Oh, I'm fine," she replied, trying to sound cheery, even though she felt the exact opposite. "How are things at the law firm? Are you still hoping to make partner this year?"

"I sure am. I've been working my fanny off in the hopes there will be a big payoff."

"I'm sure it will, Julia. You have the drive and the ambition," Avery said. "Listen, I was hoping you could do me a favor."

"Anything for a soror."

"Well, I am in need of a private investigator with absolute discretion and I was hoping you might know of someone." Given her parents' social standing in the community, she didn't want word of this leaking out.

"Is everything all right, Avery? Are you in some kind of trouble?" Julia asked. "If so, you know I'll help any way I can."

"No, no. It's nothing like that. It's nothing criminal. I just need some information."

"All right, let me get his number out of my Black-Berry." Julia paused for several moments before returning to the line. "His name is Woody Owen. He's my go-to guy. If someone is hiding something, he'll find it. And Woody will treat you with the utmost confidentiality."

"Excellent," Avery said. "He's just what I need."

Ten minutes later, she had an appointment to meet with Mr. Owen at his office near the courthouse later that day.

The rest of the afternoon, Avery was as jittery as a cat. She was dying to meet Woody, since walk-in traffic was slow at the gallery, but Hunter was watching her like a hawk. Avery was admiring several abstract paintings when Quentin Davis walked in.

What is he doing here? Avery wondered. Every time she was around him for longer than a few minutes, he threw her off balance, and she didn't need that today, so she hid behind a wall to prevent him from seeing her.

She watched and admired the man from afar. He

exuded raw sex appeal even from across the room. She didn't know if it was his glistening bald head or the way his jeans hung low to his well-shaped posterior. All she knew was that she was attracted to him and that would never do. He was all wrong for her. She preferred the clean-cut, suit-and-tie type. So what was it about Quentin Davis that caused her to get all hot and bothered?

Avery didn't take the time to find out. She scurried off to the ladies' room to bring down her rapid pulse and to check her appearance. She smoothed her ponytail and bangs, straightened her diamond heart necklace and checked her lipstick. Satisfied that she looked presentable, Avery exited the restroom and walked toward the front of the gallery. She found Quentin leaning over the reception desk speaking with the intern they'd recently hired.

She stopped a few feet from their little tête-à-tête and waited to be acknowledged. Quentin finally glanced in her direction and when he did, Avery nearly froze in place, her breath catching in her throat as he rewarded her with a disarming smile.

"Avery." Quentin straightened and strolled toward her. "Just the person I was looking for." He had decided to make a spur-of-the-moment stop at the Henri Lawrence Gallery. He hadn't forgotten the bet, and it was time he paid it due attention.

"Oh, why was that?" Avery asked, trying to sound nonchalant.

"Well…" Quentin started, but then stopped in front of a painting. "This is an excellent piece of abstract work, don't you think? I love the artist's use of color and form."

"Yes, I agree. Forbes has an amazing gift for depicting objects in an unconventional way, but I doubt you came all this way to discuss art," Avery replied, glancing sideways at Quentin.

"No, I didn't." He shifted his gaze to Avery. He allowed his eyes to travel from her conservative pumps, her black wide-leg pants up to her crisp white shirt and black vest.

Avery tried hard to keep her eyes on the painting, but with the way Quentin was staring at her, she found it difficult to remain focused.

"I came to ask you to dinner."

"Dinner?"

"Yes, you know, it's called a date when two people agree to share a meal at the same table." Quentin laughed as he spoke.

"I know what a date is," Avery replied tersely.

"Perhaps you haven't been on one in a while?" he asked. "If so, I'd like to remedy that."

"Just because we agreed to be civil doesn't mean I'd agree to share dinner with you," she responded.

"Please don't tell me we're back to square one again? I thought we agreed to be friends and if so, you can look on this as a friendly dinner."

Avery was about to answer when Hunter came

toward them. "Hunter, I'd like you to meet Quentin Davis." Avery relished the thought of changing the subject.

"Mr. Davis," Hunter said. "It's a pleasure to have you at the gallery." Hunter hadn't realized that he was the world-renowned photographer when he'd crashed Gabriel's showing.

Quentin glanced at the interloper. He didn't appreciate his conversation with Avery being interrupted. "Thank you. And you are?" He was trying to make headway with the beautiful diva.

"Hunter Garrett, the director of the gallery."

Avery watched Hunter puff out his chest as if he were some big dog and extend his hand. She despised Hunter's posturing. He didn't hold a candle to Quentin's naturally broad chest.

"Pleasure to meet you, Hunter," Quentin said, shaking his hand. Then a mischievous thought popped into his head. He could use Hunter to help him on his mission. "I was just asking Ms. Roberts to dinner so that we could discuss the possibility of exhibiting some of my work."

"Would you really be interested in exhibiting in a gallery as small as ours?" Hunter asked.

Avery gave Quentin the evil eye. She knew exactly what he was up to. He was using her job as a way to get her to go out with him. She could strangle him!

"I could be persuaded over dinner if Avery would

agree to accompany me," Quentin said open-endedly. He couldn't disguise the glint of humor in his eyes as he smiled at Avery. He could see the wheels turning in her head and knew she could spit nails at him, but he suspected she would do the right thing.

Hunter whirled around and glared at Avery. When she didn't speak up, Hunter spoke for her. "I'm sure Avery would love to join you for dinner to discuss an exhibition. Wouldn't you, Avery?"

She feigned a polite smile and said what was expected. Especially since her boss was present. "Of course, HLG would be honored to have someone of your caliber exhibit here."

"Excellent," Hunter said, leaving the duo. "I'll leave you to the details."

Once Hunter was no longer within earshot, Avery glared daggers at Quentin. "How dare you use my job as a weapon against me?"

"It was the only way I could get you to agree," Quentin fired back. "And who knows, you just might enjoy a night out."

"I doubt that, but seeing as I don't have much choice…where should I meet you for this grand date?"

"Why don't I pick you up?"

"Oh no, I'm not giving you my address so you can show up at my apartment unannounced any time you feel like it. No, thank you." Avery crossed her arms stubbornly.

Quentin inched closer to her until their faces were inches apart. "Why must you challenge me on everything? Why can't you just let me be a man and pick you up like a regular date? Or do you get a kick out of being a shrew?"

Avery stepped back. What she didn't like was how vulnerable she felt whenever she was around him. "No, I don't get a kick out of it. You just happen to bring out the worst in me," she huffed. "But I suppose you can pick me up."

She sauntered over to the reception desk, giving Quentin a delicious view of her derriere as she swished in front of him. She quickly scribbled her address and handed him the Post-it.

Their fingers touched when he accepted the note. Quentin felt a spark and he was sure Avery had to feel it, too, even though her expression revealed nothing. "Thank you." He grinned. "That wasn't so difficult, was it?" When she didn't reply, Quentin said, "I'll see you at seven on Friday."

Once the door had shut behind him, Avery exhaled. She hadn't realized she'd been holding her breath the entire time.

Chapter 4

Avery told Hunter that she had a doctor's appointment later that afternoon, so she could meet with Woody Owen. Hunter wasn't too happy about it, but Avery couldn't care less. She needed answers.

Woody's office was nothing like what Avery had imagined. She'd expected a private investigator's office to be chaos and disorder like in the movies. Instead, she found a modern decor and abstract artwork lining the walls. And she was even further off the mark with Woody. He had a shock of white hair, a big grin and was casually dressed in a polo shirt and khaki trousers. He looked like a grandfather rather than a hard-nosed detective, and he sure didn't mince words either.

"Have you thought about why you're doing this?" he asked.

"Of course, or I wouldn't be here," Avery returned sarcastically. "I need to know my roots, if only for medical conditions. What if I have kids one day?"

"All right, then, I'm not going to sugarcoat this for you, Ms. Roberts. You have a long road ahead of you. Months, possibly years. Your original birth certificate that has your biological mother's name has been sealed, so if she hasn't registered with an agency or signed a consent form to release her identity, then it's going to be an uphill battle to find her. Do you understand what I'm telling you?"

"Yes." Avery nodded.

"First thing we need to do is gather as much information as we can," he said. "Such as your date of birth, the state in which you were born and the state where your adoption was finalized and most importantly what agency arranged your adoption."

"What do you mean, date of birth? I was born on November 3rd," Avery replied haughtily.

"Possibly, or perhaps you were born several days before," he responded. "We just can't be sure. We have to check a few days before and after your birth date."

"Ohmigod!" Avery shook her head. Even her birth date could be a lie? "This is a nightmare."

"I know this seems daunting," Woody said, trying to calm her down from behind his desk, "but we may get lucky. You just never know in these situations. My advice is to talk to your parents and find out as much information as you can."

Her parents! They were the last people Avery wanted to see. Right now, she didn't want to have anything to do with them.

"I know you're angry," Woody said, "but they're our best bet."

"Thank you for your time." Avery stood and shook Woody's hand. She appreciated his forthrightness. "I'll be in touch."

After she left his office, all she wanted to do was cry. She wanted to crawl up into a burrow like a groundhog and not come out until spring. Whether she wanted to or not, she was going to have to contact her parents if she wanted more details on her adoption, which was an unpleasant task and one she was not looking forward to.

When her father called mid-week, Avery had no choice but to accept his lunch invitation. She hoped he would be able to shed some light on her adoption and provide cold hard facts that she could forward to Woody. These thoughts rumbled through Avery's mind as she met her father at the Lenox Room.

Painted in deep reds and oranges, with cozy chairs and incandescent lighting, the restaurant had a very relaxed atmosphere, which was probably why her father had chosen it.

Prompt as always, Avery found him already seated at a table for two and dressed in a three-piece suit. He looked handsome even with a receding hairline. "Avery, I'm so glad you agreed to see me." Her father stood up as she approached.

When he leaned over and placed a light kiss on her cheek, Avery flinched as if burned and quickly sat down. It was hard to believe that the man she'd adored her entire life was not a blood relation. She'd always been Daddy's little girl.

"I know you're angry with me and your mother," he began.

"Please, Dad." Avery put up a hand to halt him from continuing. "That's the understatement of the year. This isn't like the time you forbid me to go to the Rolling Stones and I didn't speak to you for a week. The wound is much deeper."

"I realize that, Avery," her father responded, "but I was hoping since you'd had several days to digest this information, you might be open to hearing our reasons why."

"What possible reason would you have for keeping the truth from me at this late date?" When he started to speak, Avery interrupted him. "Don't answer that. I bet you it was Mother. Wasn't it? She was the one who made you continue this farce?"

"No." Her father shook his head. "*We* both agreed it was for the best."

"Do you honestly expect me to believe that, Dad?

I know Mother. I know what she's like. Heaven forbid I see her as less than the perfect wife and mother." Appearances were everything to Veronica Roberts.

"That's true, she's not perfect," her father acquiesced. "She's human and as much as she'd like to think she's perfect, she's not because humans make mistakes."

"So that's it?" Avery asked, her voice rising. "That's it? I'm supposed to just sweep this under the rug to spare Mother's feelings. Well, I won't do that, Dad, and you can't expect me to."

"I don't, sweetheart. I just expect you to listen and have an open mind."

"Okay, fine. I'm listening." Avery settled back in her chair.

"Well…" her father started. "Initially, we had every intention of telling you the truth when you were old enough to understand."

"Did you ever try, Dad?"

Clayton Roberts nodded his head. "Yes, we did. You were eight and all the kids at school were questioning why you looked different from your mother and me."

Avery remembered that all too vividly. Young children could be cruel, and they had made fun of her light complexion and her funny-looking tiger eyes, as they'd called them. They'd always asked her why she was so light while her parents were the color of rich caramel. "And as I recall," Avery said, "you lied and told me that Mother's great-great grandmother was mulatto."

"Yes, we did, because by that point, we'd come to see you as our own flesh and blood, so much so that the truth began to matter less and less. And once we made that choice, there was no going back."

"That does not excuse the lies." Avery refused to let him off the hook that easily. "I'm old enough to understand, Dad. And I want the whole truth and nothing but, starting with names and places."

"Why?"

She didn't hesitate to answer. "Because I'm going to find my biological parents, starting with my birth mother."

"You can't!" her father shouted across the table. Several patrons looked up, so he lowered his voice. "Avery, you can't do this."

"I'm not asking your permission," she said. "I am going to find them with or without you, but I was hoping it would be the former."

"I don't know, Avery." Her father's head hung low. "If your mother ever found out, this would hurt her terribly."

"I'm sorry, Dad. Really, I am, but this can't be avoided. I need to know where I come from if nothing else than for medical purposes. What if I ever have some kids someday? I need to know my family's medical history."

Her father sighed. Avery could tell he was wrestling with some internal demons, but without his help, it would be a lot harder for Woody to unearth the truth, if ever, and it would take a whole lot longer. "Well?" Wide-eyed, Avery peered into her father's dark brown eyes. "What's it going to be?"

After a long pause, he finally answered. "All right. I'll help you, but your mother's not going to like this." Clayton Roberts was certain of that fact. Veronica was going to hit the roof when she found out. And now was definitely not the time to tell her; she was already so distraught from this secret coming out. Clayton doubted she could take hearing that Avery was searching for her biological parents.

Avery nodded. "What I need to know is the name of the agency you and Mom used. And who oversaw my adoption." She pulled out a legal pad, ready to take down some notes.

Over the next hour, her father informed her that Peter Gallagher, an attorney and close family friend, had handled her adoption. Avery discovered she had not been born in Manhattan as her birth certificate indicated. She'd actually been born and officially adopted in New Hampshire. Her parents had picked her up hours after the delivery. Apparently, her biological mother hadn't wanted to see her for fear she might never be able to give her up. Avery was disturbed that she had handed her daughter off to Clayton and Veronica Roberts without ever seeing her baby girl.

After lunch, Avery thanked her father for his openness and honesty. She knew it was difficult for him to do the exact opposite of what her mother would want, but Avery assured him that he'd done the right thing. She even responded to his hug upon leaving and told him she'd be in touch if she found out any news. They both agreed to keep this information to themselves until Avery found out anything substantial. Why upset her mother unnecessarily?

When she called Woody on her way back to the gallery, he informed her that New Hampshire was a state that permitted adoptees over the age of eighteen to receive a non-certified copy of their original birth certificate. So Avery made a pit stop by his office to copy her driver's license and fill out the necessary application form required by the Vital Records Department, along with a permission note that Woody's secretary notarized, which would allow Woody to receive the documentation. Once she gained access to her original birth certificate, then Woody would have somewhere to begin his search.

When she arrived back at the gallery, a long black stretch limousine was parked outside. Inside, she found Hunter with the owner of the gallery, and from the looks of it, Hunter was giving Mr. Lawrence an earful.

"Hunter, Mr. Lawrence." Avery nodded to the two men.

"How are you, Ms. Roberts?" Henri inquired.

"I'm well, thank you," she said, peering at him. Henri was an attractive Asian man with spiky moussed hair and a goatee. He possessed an aura of wealth, power and privilege.

"I was just telling Mr. Lawrence the results of Gabriel's showing the other night," Hunter said. "We did remarkably well, considering it was his first show."

Considering he was my find, thought Avery.

"Yes, we sold ten paintings," she chimed in.

"Eleven to be exact," Hunter corrected. "We had someone stop by early today while you were at lunch and purchase another great piece."

Was that yet another dig at her? So she'd had a long lunch. What harm was there in that? Hunter was quite able to handle the gallery in her absence. He was director, after all.

"That's wonderful news," Henri said. "Keep up the good work." He patted Hunter on the shoulder. "I knew I made the right decision when I chose you to helm this location."

Avery despised the old boys' club. She was quite capable of doing Hunter's job as well as he did, if not better. Although he was above her, Avery did all the hard work, but he got all the glory. She supposed that was the downside of being second in command.

"Well, I'm off to the airport for my fifteen-day Mediterranean cruise," Henri boasted. "I'll see you both in a few weeks."

"Enjoy." Avery put on a fake smile and waved as he left.

Once the door was closed, Hunter turned and faced Avery. "Where were you?" he asked. "That was an awfully long lunch."

"I had some personal business to attend to," Avery replied.

"You've had a lot of personal business to attend to the last couple of days, Avery. Are you looking for another position?"

"Why? Should I be?" She raised a brow.

"I don't know. That depends. If you can't keep your focus on your job, then perhaps you should think about becoming a society woman like your mother. You don't even need to work like the rest of us."

"How dare you?" Avery returned haughtily. "Just because I grew up privileged does not mean I'm above hard work. Clearly, you know that by now."

"What I know is what I see. And what I see is that you've been distracted," Hunter said, "and that's all I'm going to say on the subject." With that comment, he turned and strode away, leaving his words dangling in the air. But Avery knew their meaning. Keep it up and she'd be pounding the pavement, looking for a new job.

Avery was nervous as she stood in the foyer of her two-bedroom Central Park West apartment waiting for Quentin. She'd taken great care to dress for the evening. She'd chosen black pants and a multi-floral blouse with a three-quarter-length sleeve as a jacket over her cami. The outfit was smart and sophisticated.

When her doorbell rang, Avery's heart lurched. She willed herself to calm down and took one final glance in the mirror before opening the door. Quentin was standing on the opposite side looking calm, cool and collected while Avery's heart raced. Her gaze inched upward from his muscular chest to his chiseled face. His gleaming bald head was underscored by his intense eyes, which were fixed on her. His broad mouth broke into a smile. "Avery."

"Quentin," she finally replied, "you're right on time." She glanced at her watch, but made no move to let him in. She could stand there all night looking at him in his faded blue jeans and crisp white shirt with three buttons casually opened at the top.

"May I come in?" Quentin asked.

"Oh, of course." Avery stepped aside to allow him to enter her apartment.

He wasn't surprised to find her place was as meticulous and orderly as the lady herself. The warm earth shades oozed class and elegance. He stepped out onto her enormous balcony and found a great view of Central Park.

"Nice place," he commented on his way back in. A little devoid of warmth, he thought, but nice all the same. He'd love to come in and spice it up with some color.

"Thank you," Avery said. She was curious as to what was roaming through his mind as he fingered the Monet, Renoir and Degas prints that adorned her walls. He was probably thinking she was uppity and a snob.

"You must love the Impressionists," Quentin said.

"Yes, I like their use of short, thick strokes, the soft edges, the intermingling colors and the way their paintings command your attention," Avery rattled on, until she realized Quentin was eyeing her up and down. "What's wrong? Do you not like what I'm wearing?"

Quentin rubbed his goatee. "It's not that…" He paused.

"Then what?" she asked, exasperated. She thought she looked just fine. She was wearing Michael Kors, after all.

He chuckled at her tone. "It's fine if we were going to a fine-dining restaurant, but for where we're going this evening, you are a tad overdressed."

"Where are we going?" Avery asked.

"To this Moroccan restaurant that I know in Jersey."

"Moroccan?" she said haughtily. She'd never tried Moroccan food. All she knew was that they used a lot of curries and chutneys.

"Yes, Moroccan," he replied, mocking her. "And I just thought you might feel more comfortable in some jeans. You know, less out of place, but it's your choice."

She thought about it for a moment. He did have a point. She doubted her black pants and multi-floral blouse would fit in. "Give me five minutes," she said and scurried off to her master suite.

It took longer than five minutes for Avery to rummage through her closet because she couldn't remember what she'd done with the single pair of jeans she owned.

Avery released a huge sigh of relief when they zipped up with ease. She glanced at her rear end in the mirror. The jeans hugged every curve, which was exactly how Quentin wanted them, she was sure. She replaced her jacket with one of Jenna's tops from her photo shoots. As a talent agent, she some-times secured free clothing from the designers and passed along what she didn't want to Avery. The sexy, low-cut top wasn't really her style, but it fit the occasion.

She breezed down the hall and found Quentin perusing a magazine on the edge of the sofa. "Will this suffice, Your Grace?" she asked, bowing in front of him.

He smiled. Avery Roberts was certainly a shrew, but if she thought her sarcastic tone would send him running in the opposite direction, she was wrong. He had a bet to win. He would show his friends that he was still a playa and, like fine wine, he had only gotten better with age.

Quentin rose to his feet and pulled Avery toward

him. "Yes, that will do," he said, mere inches from her face. He loved the slight bit of décolletage he'd received when she'd bowed.

The breath caught in Avery's throat and for a second she thought he was going to kiss her, but instead he stepped away, leaving her bereft and wishing he had.

"Ready?" he asked.

"Yes," she huffed, reached for her purse on the console in the foyer and preceded him out the door. Quentin smiled as he watched her switch. He definitely liked the way she looked in those jeans. She'd been anticipating that he was going to kiss her, but instead he'd wait and when she was panting for it, he would give it to her and give it to her good.

Chapter 5

Once they exited her building, Avery looked up and down the street for a taxicab, ignoring the motorcycle parked directly in front of her apartment building.

"You don't have to worry about one of those," Quentin said, walking to the Harley.

"Why is that?" she asked.

"Because we're taking this," he said, hopping on the back of the bike.

Avery's eyes grew wide with fear as she walked to the curb. "Surely you jest. There's no way I'm getting on that death trap."

"I'm not asking," Quentin said, throwing her a helmet. "Get on."

"Oh no!" She shook her head vehemently. She'd heard about people getting seriously injured or worse.

"Don't make me get off this bike and physically put you on it," he warned.

"I've never been on a motorcycle before. What if I fall off?"

"Then I guess you had better hold on real tight, now, hadn't you?" Quentin chuckled. When Avery didn't move a muscle, he got off and walked around the bike. "There's nothing to be afraid of. I'm a good driver and we have helmets to protect us." He took the helmet out of Avery's shaking hands and placed it over her head.

"My hair," she said when he snapped the helmet in place.

"It'll be fine." Quentin helped her onto the bike. "I promise I'll take good care of you." He hopped back onto the bike and turned on the ignition.

Reluctantly, she wrapped her arms around his middle. "You'd better!" Avery yelled over the roar of the engine.

"Hold on," Quentin said as they took off down the road.

She held on for dear life. On the forty-minute drive from Manhattan to Parsippany, New Jersey, Avery prayed. She didn't know why she'd allowed herself to be bullied into getting on this contraption. She must be mad. When they finally stopped at a small strip mall, she drew a long-overdue deep breath.

Quentin jumped off and took off his helmet. "Are you all right?" he asked, because Avery had had a death grip on him the entire way and he'd barely been able to breathe.

"I'm okay, I think," Avery replied.

After she removed her helmet, Quentin secured it on the bike and grabbed her by the hand, "C'mon, you'll love this place. They have a live Moroccan band and belly dancers."

"Belly dancers!" Avery exclaimed.

The restaurant's large wooden doors opened up into a warm atmosphere with hand-painted murals and a fabric-draped ceiling. The red-and-orange color scheme was a tribute to the many images she'd seen of Morocco and was nothing like any other restaurant she'd ever frequented in New York.

They were ushered into a large open room where they were seated with other guests on banquettes strewn with ornate pillows. Avery was surprised that there weren't any tables. Handmade, intricately designed circular gold trays served as their tabletop. Before the meal arrived, a waiter dressed in traditional Moroccan clothing brought over a *tasse* and a basin, and set them on the small round wooden table.

"What's that for?" Avery asked.

"It's for us to wash our hands."

"Whatever for?"

"Because we eat with our hands," Quentin returned, rolling up his sleeves.

"That's completely uncivilized." She was used to eating with utensils.

"It's the Moroccan custom. And as they say… when in Rome…" Quentin dipped his hands in the water. "C'mon, don't be such a spoilsport."

He was glad when Avery finally joined her hands with his in the basin. Quentin poured water over her hands with his and although it was a purely innocent gesture, it was highly sensual. And to make matters worse, the restaurant was so crowded, she and Quentin had to sit so closely their thighs touched. It made Avery completely aware of him at her side. She finally had to ask, "Why did you bring me here?"

"Because I wanted you to try someplace different. Take you out of your comfort zone."

"Why?" she asked, drying her hands with a towel the waiter had left.

"Because, my dear—" Quentin tucked a loose strand of hair behind her ear "—you need to live a little."

"I am very cultured," Avery replied, somewhat offended by his offhanded comment.

"Why must you be so combative? I just wanted to show you something different. Can't you let me do that?"

Her eyes narrowed and he thought she was going

to say no, but she smiled instead and said, "Yes. So, what are we having for dinner? Because I have no idea what to order."

Quentin ordered items for them both to share, so Avery could try several of his favorite foods on the menu.

While the waiter put their order in, Quentin used the time to learn more about Avery. He found she was a lot more open-minded than he'd thought and enjoyed many of the same things that he did. She had an affinity not just for art, but the theater, literature, classical music and travel. She was well traveled and had seen her share of Europe.

"Have you ever been to the Middle East?" Quentin inquired.

"No, I haven't," Avery replied. "I'm sure you have some interesting stories you could tell. I saw your Iraq photographs in *Time* and they were amazing. You captured the despair and fear in the country."

"You have no idea the horrors and atrocities that soldiers face when they go to war. It's brutal. No wonder many of them come back traumatized. My photographs capture only a second of the things they see and experience daily."

"Are you going back any time soon?"

Quentin shook his head. "No, as much as I enjoy life abroad, I'd like to stay on American soil for a while. And plus, I kind of like the sights right here in New York." He glanced at her sideways.

Avery blushed because Quentin was in no way hiding his obvious interest in her.

"Did I say something wrong?" he asked, inching closer to her.

"Uh…no," she said. "It's just that you and I…"

"Have more in common than you realized," Quentin finished.

He was right, but she wasn't about to admit that. "No, what I was about to say is that we've lived totally different lives. I was brought up in a cocoon on Park Avenue, sheltered from the horrors of the world, except what I see on the news. While you've seen them. Lived them. I'm sure that had to change you."

"Yes, it has," Quentin said and reached for her hand. He held her small delicate hand in his large one. "It's made me value life and all it has to offer."

Despite their differences, Avery felt a pull toward Quentin and had it not been for the waiter returning with their hummus appetizer on a beautifully decorated platter, she might have fallen into his arms.

"What is it?" Avery asked, looking at the strange mixture.

The waiter answered, "It's a combination of chickpeas, tahini, spices and olive oil. Please try it."

"Here." Quentin grabbed a piece of flat bread and dipped it in the smooth, creamy mixture. He leaned over and brought the bread to Avery's lips. "C'mon, don't be a chicken."

She opened her mouth and took the plunge. She

bit into it and found the hummus to be surprisingly tasty.

"So, what do you think?" he asked, licking the remnants off his fingertips.

Avery turned and smiled at Quentin. "It's not bad. Actually, it's quite good."

"I'm glad you like it." They continued their seven-course Moroccan journey when he offered her another delicacy, *bastilla.* Crisp phyllo leaves powdered with cinnamon and confectioner's sugar enclosed the delicate, juicy filling of saffron chicken. It was completely sensual having Quentin feed her, and not just because it was a mouthwatering blend of tastes and aromas, but because of the way Quentin looked at her. His gaze was a soft caress across her face and Avery had to admit she enjoyed the attention.

They continued their meal with *harira,* a traditional Moroccan lentil soup, and a tabbouleh salad of couscous, tomato, herbs and olive oil.

"I've never had anything quite like this," Avery admitted when they were halfway through their entrée of slowly braised baby lamb *tagine* served with saffron rice. "Thank you," she said when they ended the extravagant meal with a plate of fruit, pastries and a cup of mint tea.

"Don't thank me yet," Quentin said when the live Moroccan band took to the stage. "The night isn't over yet."

Avery turned her head at the exact moment the

belly dancer came sashaying into the room. Avery had no idea how she could shake and gyrate her hips with such ease. There was no way *she* could do that. Or so she thought.

The dancer made her way around the room, asking several patrons to join her in the native ritual. When she made her way to their banquette, Quentin pointed to Avery. "She'd love to dance."

"Unh-unh." Avery vehemently shook her head. "I don't belly dance."

"It is easy," the woman said with a thick Moroccan accent. "Come, I will show you." She pulled Avery to her feet and before Avery knew it, the woman had wrapped a large piece of fabric around her hips.

Standing, Avery noticed all eyes in the restaurant were on her as the Moroccan woman placed her hands on Avery's hips and showed her the movements in quick succession. Avery tried to follow suit, but found that belly dancing was not her forte. As she was sure Quentin had suspected. When she turned and attempted to gyrate her body to the live music like the dancer, she found Quentin's hot and hungry gaze fixed on her. Everyone in the restaurant clapped enthusiastically, cheering her on.

Quentin, meanwhile, was having great fun watching Avery give belly dancing her best effort. She wasn't inept, but she wasn't great either. If his friends could see her now, he highly doubted they'd be calling her an ice queen. Despite her initial objections to his mode of transportation and choice of restaurant, Avery had come through like a real trooper. She'd shown that she could let down her hair and it made Quentin admire her courage.

Afterward, Avery took a bow and returned to her seat. "How was I?" she asked breathlessly.

Ever the gentleman, Quentin lied right through his teeth. "You were great."

"Liar," Avery said, smiling at him. "I'm going to kill you for this, Quentin Davis," she whispered in his ear.

"I look forward to it," he whispered back.

They left the restaurant shortly thereafter and headed back to New York. At a stoplight, Avery nudged him, lifted her faceplate and asked, "What's next?" She was sure Quentin had something else up his sleeve.

"It wouldn't be a surprise if I told you, now, would it?" he asked.

An hour later found Quentin parking his Harley outside a small club. "You'll never believe who's playing here tonight."

"Who?"

"John Mayer. He doesn't do small venues like this anymore, but because he got his start in places like this, occasionally he'll play in one. C'mon, I think his set is about to start."

He rushed Avery inside the small club. She

wouldn't have suspected Quentin was the type to listen to acoustic soft rock, more like rhythm and blues and hip-hop. Quentin continued to surprise her at every turn with his eclectic range of tastes.

The hour-and-a-half concert was on point. John Mayer sang his hits "Your Body Is A Wonderland," "Why Georgia" and "No Such Thing." Throughout the concert, Quentin never strayed far from Avery's side. If she wanted a drink, he was right there. If she was grooving to the music, he was right behind her with his arms casually wrapped around her waist as he swayed with her.

Quentin noticed that Avery didn't object when his arms encircled her. He was definitely making progress. When Mayer sang a ballad, Quentin turned Avery toward him and they danced nice and slow.

Avery didn't realize just how much she'd been enjoying Quentin's company until the date was over. He'd stirred emotions she'd never felt before.

"Thank you for a wonderful evening," Avery said when they finally made their way back to her apartment building. Hopping off the back of the bike, she handed Quentin his helmet.

"You're welcome," he said as he turned off the ignition. He swung his leg over the bike and locked both the helmets in place.

"Have a good night," Avery said and started to walk away, but Quentin said, "Wait!"

He quickly spun her around and before she real-

ized what was happening, his lips were on hers—and
they weren't unwelcome. Instead, they felt warm
and inviting. Quentin's kiss was slow and addictive.
It was like a drug she couldn't get enough of and
needed a hit from. When his tongue thrust hot and
masterfully into her mouth and persuaded her into a
duel, Avery responded with equal ardor. His hands,
meanwhile, scorched a trail as they skimmed her
throat and the fullness of her breasts.

When he released her from his embrace, Avery
had to touch her lips because she felt as if he'd
branded her as his.

"You must have really needed that," Quentin said.

"Why would you say that?" she asked, haughtily
taking a step backward.

"Because you kiss like you're making love. You
have no idea how erotic that is." Quentin couldn't
remember the last time a woman had kissed him
with such abandon. There had been raw emotion
behind that kiss and it had surprised the heck out of
him.

"Really?" Avery's cheeks turned red. No one had
ever told her that before. In fact, most men had said
she was too reserved and needed to let go. Perhaps
it was not her kissing technique, but the man himself
who had brought out the passion in her? The knowledge made her heart pound in her chest. Could he
hear its frantic beat?

"Yes, really." Quentin smiled broadly. "If you

kiss me like that again, I might have to take you back up to your apartment and ravish you all night." He was sure she had to have felt the bold evidence of his arousal pressed against her.

"Ravish me?" Avery laughed. "Quentin, do women really fall for lines like that?"

He chuckled and rubbed his chin thoughtfully. "Sometimes. Yes."

She couldn't stop from grinning. She had a feeling he wasn't lying. There was definitely something about Quentin Davis that intrigued her more than any man had in a long time. She didn't want to be attracted, but there was no escaping his sheer magnetism. Or the fact that he was intelligent, sexy as hell and funny, too. "Thank you again for a lovely evening, but it's late."

"Fair enough." Quentin leaned down and lightly swept his lips over hers again. "Perhaps we can do this again?"

"Maybe," Avery replied. She didn't want to give a player like Quentin a big head and let him think he'd completely won her over—when in fact he already had. "Good night," she said over her shoulder before entering her apartment building.

As the door closed behind her, Quentin shook his head. Avery Roberts was not going to cut him any slack. She was too stubborn to admit that she'd felt an attraction during that kiss just as much as he had. Avery Roberts had certainly piqued his curiosity. So much so, he now wanted to see where this would lead and not just for the bet. There was a lioness just waiting to be unleashed underneath that cool exterior.

"Oh, there's no maybe, Avery," Quentin said. "We'll be seeing each other again real soon."

"You sounded strange when you called and said we *had* to meet," Jenna said when she met up with Avery for lunch on Saturday.

"Jenna, I wouldn't know where to start." Should she begin with the fact that she'd been adopted? Or that she was attracted to Quentin Davis?

"Why don't you try? Talking it out always helps," Jenna said. "Is it your job? Is Hunter acting like a jerk?"

Avery shook her head. She wished it were as simple as that, but it wasn't. "Hunter's always a jerk."

"What, then?"

Avery decided to start with the former. "I'm adopted."

"What?" Jenna's eyes grew wide. "Are you serious?"

"Most definitely, I wouldn't joke about this. When I was helping my mother clean out the attic, I found my adoption papers and a copy of what turns out to be my amended birth certificate."

"No." Jenna was shocked. "Are you sure, Avery?

I mean you're thirty-three years old. Why wouldn't they have told you?"

"I have no idea, Jenna. When I saw the word *adoption* written on those pages, I didn't know what to think, but they admitted it. They've lied to me my entire life."

"Oh, Avery, I'm so sorry." Jenna hugged her best friend. "No wonder you haven't returned my calls. You must be so devastated. What can I do?"

"There's nothing that can be done, Jenna." Avery had had time to process the news and to take action, such as trying to find her biological parents.

"Then a drink is definitely in order," Jenna replied. When a waiter walked by, she tapped him on the shoulder. "Waiter, we'll have two cosmos, please." She turned back around. "So, what's next?"

"I've hired a private investigator to look for my biological mother."

The waiter returned with two large martinis and placed them on the table. Avery was the first to reach for hers and sipped generously.

"How long does he think it'll take to find her?"

"Who knows?" Avery shrugged. "Months, possibly years."

"I'm so sorry, Avery." Jenna reached across the table and placed her hand over hers. "Let's talk about something else then, you know, take your mind off things."

"How about we start with my date with Quentin Davis?"

"Your date? Since when?" Jenna didn't recall Avery mentioning anything about a date with that gorgeous photographer.

"Since last night." Avery blushed, lowering her lashes.

"And?" Jenna was dying for details. She couldn't believe reserved Avery would actually go out of her comfort zone and date a hottie like Quentin Davis.

"Believe it or not, I had a lot of fun," Avery said.

"What did you do?"

"We went to a Moroccan restaurant where we ate with our hands, if you can believe it?" Avery held up her pristine French-manicured nails. "My hands, Jenna," Avery said in disbelief. "And then he took me to a John Mayer concert."

"Wow, that sounds like an incredible first date." Jenna's brow furrowed. "I'm jealous. So, how did it end?"

Avery closed her eyes for a moment and remembered the way his lips had moved over hers, coaxing a response from her. And the battery of sensations that had assailed her at the slightest graze of his hands on her breasts. Her eyes flew open immediately and she found Jenna staring at her.

"It must have been some ending!" Jenna replied to Avery's wistful expression.

"It certainly was." Avery smiled.

Chapter 6

"So, are you ready to get back to work?" Quentin's agent, Jason Morgan, asked when Quentin stopped by his office in Midtown for his next assignment.

"No, not really," Quentin replied. After three weeks off, he'd gotten rather used to his carefree days. "But I suppose I couldn't stay on vacation forever."

"No, you can't. *Capitalist* has been chomping at the bit for you to do a photo exposé."

"Who's it on?" Quentin asked.

"See for yourself." Jason slid a manila folder across his desk. Quentin picked it up and flipped it open.

"Holy…" Quentin gasped. He was caught off

guard by the contents of the folder. *Richard King* was his next assignment. *Capitalist* wanted him to follow King for a few weeks and reveal the man behind the multi-million-dollar King Corporation.

"What's wrong?" Jason asked. He was disturbed by his client's reaction to what was considered a great opportunity to showcase his talents.

Quentin stared speechlessly at the folder for several moments before handing it back to Jason. "I can't accept that job."

"Why the hell not? *Capitalist* will pay you a mint for your photographs."

Quentin shook his head. "I can't, Jason."

"Until you give me a reason, Q, I can't help you."

Quentin rose to his feet and walked over to the floor-to-ceiling window. "You have no idea how messy this can get. Richard King is the man trying to take over the community center where Malik, Sage, Dante and I grew up. His corporation is trying to destroy the community."

Understanding dawned on Jason and he rubbed his chin thoughtfully. "And your friends have come to you for help?"

"Yes. And I agreed to use all my resources to help stop this travesty. How can I do that if I'm spotlighting the very man who's a symbol of everything they're against?"

"Because I already committed you," Jason said. "I'm sorry, Quentin, but I had no idea."

Quentin spun around and his dark eyebrows slanted into a frown. "Well, you're just going to have to un-commit me, Jason."

"I can't. I've already cashed the advance. And anyway, it would be completely unprofessional. Quentin, I told you about this job weeks ago and you agreed. I can't go back and tell them you're not available. If I'd known this when you got back, I would have told them to look elsewhere. It's crunch time now."

Quentin understood where Jason was coming from, but money wasn't everything to him. He would be well off with or without this assignment. "There are any number of qualified photographers out there, Jason."

"They don't want another *qualified* photographer, Q," Jason said. "They want you. You're the best. And Richard King requested you," he added for good measure.

"Now you're yanking my chain."

Jason laughed. He couldn't kid a kidder. "Okay, perhaps that was laying it on a little thick, but go meet Richard King and if you decide you don't want to do the story, come back and I'll see what I can do."

"I don't know…." Quentin had a bad feeling in the pit of his stomach.

"Perhaps if you meet the man, you might be able to sway him."

"Away from a multimillion-dollar investment? That's highly unlikely, but I'll go," Quentin said, much to Jason's relief. He wanted to meet the tycoon who thought he could ride roughshod over an entire community without anyone fighting back.

"Thank you," Jason said. "It'll all work out. You'll see."

Quentin shrugged. He doubted it. Matter of fact, he was sure the you-know-what was about to hit the fan.

When he arrived at the community center later that afternoon for his first photography session with the young men from the basketball court, Malik was there waiting for him. He'd arranged for Quentin to use one of the spare rooms.

"Quentin, what's up, my brother?" Malik said, giving him a customary hug.

"Just here to show these young men the basics," Quentin said, opening up the box of cameras he'd brought with him. He'd brought each of the boys a digital camera for their own personal use. He'd also brought some of his own equipment to show them the fundamentals of photography.

"Quentin, you didn't have to do that," Malik replied.

"I wanted to—now get out of here." Quentin pushed him toward the door. "I have work to do."

As the nine boys filed in, Quentin went on to explain some essentials. "As some of you may or may not know, there are different types of cameras. I use a point-and-shoot 35 mm camera, but today many photographers have moved to digital photography that you can manipulate and edit. And I've brought some with me, one for each of you." Quentin handed them each a camera. The boys were amazed. Many of them had never been given anything so extravagant.

"Is it ours to keep?" one boy asked.

"It sure is," Quentin replied.

Afterward, he gave them their first assignment and asked them to take pictures of their family, friends and community, or whatever meant something to them. In a couple of weeks he would come back, bring his laptop and they could share their experience with the rest of the group.

"I have to admit, Q, I wasn't sure you were going to come through," Malik said as the young men exited.

Quentin frowned and stepped back. "Why not?"

"You're an important man. I wouldn't think you would have time to mess around with a bunch of kids."

"Well, you're wrong," Quentin replied, turning around. "Those kids were me. Could have been me if Mr. Webster hadn't stepped in. Listen, Malik, I know I've been away for a while, but have you really forgotten who I am?" The way Malik was talking sounded as if he had lost faith in Quentin.

"I'm sorry. I really didn't mean that how it sounded. I just meant that I'm happy those boys have a positive influence like you in their life. They need it." Malik smiled. Quentin had surprised him with his compassion. He hadn't thought that would be possible after more than twenty years of friendship, but it was. Malik couldn't be prouder of Quentin.

"And I'm happy to be here," Quentin said. And he meant it. Even though he was between a rock and a hard place professionally, he wouldn't abandon the commitment he'd made to these young men.

"I have good news," Woody said when he called Avery a couple of days later.

"You do?" Avery's voice broke mid-sentence. "Hold on a sec." She was in the middle of a sale and had to excuse herself before she could continue. She motioned to her intern to keep the client busy. "I'll be right back," she whispered to the customer and quickly rushed up the stairs to her office and closed the door. "Okay, go ahead."

"Vital Records just faxed me over a copy of your original birth certificate."

"Wow!" Avery fell back into her chair. She couldn't believe her ears. It had only been a week. She'd thought it would take much longer to receive an original copy of her birth certificate. She'd done some research on the Internet and she'd read that it took adoptees years to find their birth parents. "It's as easy as that?"

"In this case, yes," Woody replied. "I am as shocked as you are." He'd thought the process would take as long as four to six weeks for them to even find the record, but to top it all off the birth mother had her signed consent on file. Either Avery was really lucky or the office wasn't that busy.

"So, wh-what's her name, Woody?" Avery asked.

"Her name was Leah Gordon."

"Leah." Avery mulled the name over in her head. "That's really pretty. What else does it say?"

"It says she was twenty years of age and that you were born in Manchester, New Hampshire," Woody answered. "I can fax you a copy if you like."

"Uh, sure," Avery said uneasily. Did she really want to see the name her birth mother had given her before she'd handed her off to her parents?

"Sure thing, Avery. Natalie's putting it on the fax now." Woody handed his secretary the document. "Now that we know her real name, we can begin the search. I'll start first in New Hampshire."

"But what if she didn't live there?"

"Then we'll have to widen our search, which could take much longer. But for now, let's run with the assumption that she's a native from New Hampshire. And if so, then it's just a matter of following her trail."

"How soon will you know something?"

"Don't know," Woody said honestly. "She could have moved or gotten married, changed her name, or the name she gave on the certificate could be a fake, but as soon as I find out anything I'll be sure and give you a call."

"Thank you, Woody." When Avery hung up, she experienced a gamut of emotions, from excitement to absolute terror at the thought of a face-to-face meeting with her birth mother. Not to mention the fact that she and her father still hadn't told her mother yet. Avery was in the process of picking up the phone when a knock resonated on her door.

She rose, walked over and opened it. She tried not to show her displeasure at finding Hunter on the other side.

"Is it true, you just walked away from a sale?" he inquired.

"Yes, it is," Avery replied. "It was just a few moments and I was just headed back down to finish the deal."

"Don't bother, I sealed the deal."

Avery sighed. Great. There went her commission because Hunter certainly wasn't going to give her a share in it. "Thank you."

"I hope that phone call was important, because it almost cost this gallery a prime sale."

"I'm sorry, but the call was important."

"What is going on with you, Roberts?" Hunter eyed her carefully. "You've been distracted. Is there something going on in your personal life? Do you need some time off?"

Avery didn't appreciate Hunter's inquisition. "If there were, I wouldn't tell you," she responded. "My personal life is just that, Hunter. Personal. And no, I don't need any time off."

She tried to sweep past him, but he halted her. She glanced down at his hand and he quickly removed it from her arm.

"Fine, you don't have to tell me anything," Hunter said in her ear, "but just know this—you had better get focused because you're on thin ice."

"I'll remember that." Avery stalked down the stairs. She didn't know why, but she was afraid to look at that fax. This was what she wanted, right? This was what she'd hired Woody to do. So why was she so scared of seeing the truth in black and white? Avery didn't know why, but she just didn't have the courage to see in print what she knew to be a reality—that she'd been given up at birth.

Later that evening, Avery did find the courage to stop avoiding her parents' home and finally speak with her mother, Veronica. It was time she told her that she was searching for her biological parents. As she opened the front door, Avery dreaded the task ahead of her.

"Mom, Dad," she called out.

"Avery." Her mother came from the back of the house, rushing toward her. "I'm so happy you came by. I've missed you so much. Knowing that you've been angry with me has been agony." Her mother gave her a big hug.

"Hello, Mother." Avery quickly patted her back and moved away.

"Darling, please come in." Her mother pulled her toward the living room and sat down on the sofa. She patted a spot next to her. "Have a seat. What's new in your life?"

"This isn't a social visit."

"I realize that, Avery," her mother said. "I know you're still very upset with me."

"That's putting it mildly. Quite frankly, I feel like I can't trust you, which is why I'm here."

Her father walked in at just that moment. "Dad." Avery rose and accepted his kiss on the cheek. Why was it so much easier for her to forgive her dad than her mother? Avery wondered. For some reason, she held her mother responsible for keeping this deception going so long. "I was just about to explain the reason for my visit."

She watched his eyes widen with concern as he sat down opposite them. "Mother," Avery began, sitting back down, "I need to tell you something and I know this may hurt, but I felt I owed it to you to tell you where my head is at."

"Whatever it is, Avery, you can just tell me," her mother stated calmly.

Avery inhaled and released a long breath before proceeding. "I've hired a private investigator to search for my birth parents and he received a copy of my original birth certificate today. Her name is Leah—"

"You did what!" Veronica Roberts rose to her feet.

"I know—" Avery began but her mother interrupted.

"How could you do this to me?" Veronica shook her head in disbelief. "To your father. We've given you a great life. Haven't we?" she asked, grasping Avery by the shoulders.

She lowered her lashes. "Well, yes, but…"

"We're your parents," Veronica cried. "Not them. Where was this Leah person when you were crying? Or teething? Where was she when you skinned your knee?"

Avery could feel her mother's anguish and it caused hot tears to roll down her cheeks. She'd known it would hurt, but she hadn't realized just how deep the cut would go. It was as if she had just sliced open a newly healed wound.

"We're the ones that clothed you. Fed you. Loved you."

"Veronica, stop it," her father said and stepped in between the two women, but her mother was relentless.

"Was Leah at your first recital? Or your graduation? Why did you do this?" her mother shouted at her.

"Because I had to," Avery wailed, defending herself from her mother's tirade. "I didn't do this to hurt you." Avery choked back the tears. "But I need to know where I came from."

"Then go." Her mother flung out her hand toward the door.

"Mother, please," Avery said, "please, don't be upset with me."

"Just go." Her mother swept past her to the doorway, but not before giving one final blow. "Go find your *birth* parents, but I promise you it will not bring you any peace. It will bring you nothing but pain. Just like the pain you've caused me." She ran up the stairs.

"What have I done?" Avery asked, lowering herself to the couch.

"You're doing what you have to," her father replied matter-of-factly. He'd known this would hurt Veronica, but Avery had her mind made up. "Your mother is hurt, but in time, she'll understand."

"I don't know if she'll ever forgive me for this, Dad," Avery said, shaking her head. "You saw her."

"In time, she will." Her father came to her side and squeezed her shoulder. "You'll see. She's just hurt now, but give her time, she'll come around."

Avery could only hope that was the case.

As Quentin walked up Fifth Avenue toward Fifty-third Street and the King Tower the next afternoon, he saw that the building was as impressive as the man himself. After his meeting with Jason earlier in the week, Quentin had done a little research on Richard King. He was a prominent businessman with over five million square feet of prime Manhattan real estate, as well as properties throughout Florida and the West Coast. He was an up-and-coming entrepreneur who could easily surpass Donald Trump if given the opportunity. Quentin wanted to meet in person the man who symbolized the establishment and everything Malik despised.

The inside of the bronze-tinted, fifty-story glass tower was every bit as magnificent as the outside. The use of marble, granite and brass throughout the complex and inside the four-level atrium that housed shops and cafés only added to its appeal.

As the elevator climbed, Quentin put on his game face. He would be professional and cordial. He didn't want Richard King to see that he had a hidden agenda. When the elevator stopped on the fiftieth floor, Quentin exited and walked up to the circular front desk.

"May I help you?" the receptionist asked.

"Yes, I'm here to see Richard King," Quentin replied. "We have a one o'clock meeting."

"Certainly, just a moment, please." She buzzed King and while he waited she brought him a bottle of mineral water. He hadn't asked for it, but he said thank you nonetheless.

After several minutes, she said, "Follow me," and led him through the King Corporation's swanky offices with plush carpeting and into Richard King's private suite. He was on the phone and motioned to Quentin to sit down.

He took a seat and placed his photography bag on the floor. Richard King was not what he'd expected. Sure, he'd seen pictures, but in person he was much shorter and didn't appear as looming a presence as the media made him out to be. In fact, from a physical standpoint, he looked rather ordinary. He was about five foot nine, medium build with dark brown hair and wearing an Italian double-breasted suit.

"Mr. Davis, sorry about that," Richard King said as he hung up the phone. "I'm sorry to have kept you waiting." He rose from behind his desk and came forward to shake Quentin's hand.

"Not a problem, Mr. King," Quentin said. "I understand you're a busy man." Once he was closer, however, Quentin noted that Richard had striking green eyes, kind of like Avery's. If Quentin were to take this assignment, he'd definitely want to get a close-up.

"When my PR person told me about you shadowing me for an interview in *Capitalist*, I told him he must be mad. I have a huge development deal going right now," Richard said, leaning against the front of his desk. "But some good PR never hurt, right?"

"Right." Quentin went along.

"Why don't you join me for lunch?" Richard asked, standing straight and buttoning his Armani jacket. "I have a business meeting that I must attend and you'll get to see me in action."

"Actually, I think that would be great." Quentin expected King to be ruthless, which would confirm his suspicions about the man. "If it's not a problem for you?"

"Not at all," Richard returned. "I have nothing to hide."

Twenty minutes later, they were seated at the tower's restaurant while Richard met with a business associate. Throughout the hour-long lunch, Quentin watched Richard negotiate a deal. He was reasonable yet shrewd. Quentin entirely expected King to intimidate the lesser man, but by the end, Richard had his opponent thinking that he'd suggested the deal to begin with and not the other way around. Afterward, Quentin had to admire King's tenacity.

When the associate had left, Richard turned to Quentin. "So, what do you think?"

"I think you played your hand very well," Quentin replied. He was intrigued by the wealthy and shrewd businessman. He wasn't nearly as ruthless as he'd thought.

"Well, it's all a matter of knowing your opponent." Richard looked him dead in the eye. "I knew he couldn't hold out for long. Getting what I wanted was inevitable."

"You're a very confident man."

"I wouldn't be where I am today if I weren't." Richard rose to his feet. "So, how long do you think this exposé is going to take?"

"That depends on your schedule." As soon as he said the words, Quentin realized there was no backing out—he'd committed himself to this project. Malik was not going to be happy.

Chapter 7

On his way to Dante's later that evening to deliver the bad news, Quentin decided he needed something pleasant to offset the dreaded task that lay ahead of him. So he dialed Avery's cell and she answered on the third ring.

"How are you, beautiful?" Quentin asked. He'd purposely waited several days before calling after their date. He didn't want to appear overzealous. If he came on too strong, Avery would bolt. If he wanted to win the bet, she had to be handled just right. And if he was lucky, those lithe limbs would soon be entangled in bed with his as he took them both over the edge.

"Hello yourself." Avery smiled on the other end of the phone. Quentin Davis was exactly the pick-me-up she needed after an emotional week.

"How's your week been?"

"Exhausting."

"How does dinner at my loft sound tomorrow night?" Quentin wanted to get Avery on his turf and then maybe, just maybe he could break through that armor of hers. What better way than a home-cooked meal prepared by his own hands to soften her up?

"Dinner at your place?" Avery wondered aloud. Was he trying to get her over to his place so he could seduce her? *Maybe you need a little seducing,* an inner voice said back. It sure had been a long time since she'd had that particular itch scratched.

"What do you say?"

"I don't know," Avery hesitated.

"I make the moistest lemon-dill salmon you'll ever taste in your life."

Avery could just hear the little devil on her shoulder, saying go ahead, live a little. Enjoy Quentin Davis. She was sure he'd be fantastic in bed. That firm, chiseled body, that luscious mouth. She licked her lips. "Okay, okay. You don't have to convince me. What time should I arrive?"

"Seven?"

"Perfect. I'll bring the wine," she said, hanging up.

Quentin smiled as he closed his phone. He had Avery Roberts exactly where he wanted her. It was too bad the same could not be said for Richard King. Quentin hated to admit it, but King had impressed him with his negotiating skills and business prowess. He doubted Malik would see it that way. There had to be a happy medium, where he could do the job he'd been paid for and help his friend.

Quentin found the gang gathered at the bar, nibbling on several of Dante's tapas.

"Q, join us," Dante said. "I've made some great new tapas that you'll love. How does some scallops in saffron cream, chicken croquettes, sautéed portobello mushrooms and some fried calamari with garlic mayonnaise sound to you?"

"Sounds wonderful as always," Quentin said, sitting down at the bar. Dante was an excellent cook and should have had his own restaurant a long time ago. Quentin focused on him and avoided looking at Malik. "Dante, can I get a Corona?"

"Sure thing." Dante pulled out a bottle from underneath the bar, popped off the top and handed it to Quentin.

"Thanks," he said, hanging his head low.

"What's up?" Sage asked, eyeing him strangely as she bit into a croquette. "You look uneasy. Is this about your date with that upper-crust chick? How'd that go by the way?"

"Ah yes." Malik turned toward Quentin. "We've all been dying to hear the details. Or maybe you're keeping mum because you struck out?" he teased.

Quentin couldn't help but smile. Now, here was a topic he was comfortable with. "Now, you should know me better than that, Malik. A smooth player like myself never strikes out."

"So you hit a home run?" Malik asked, raising an eyebrow.

Quentin paused for effect while his friends waited for his answer. "Please, Malik. You should know me better than that."

"Than what?" Malik asked.

"I knocked it out of the ballpark," Quentin boasted.

"You're still the man!" Malik raised his hand and Quentin high-fived him.

"I knew it," Sage said and shook her head. "You are still every bit the playa you were when you left five years ago. So did you sleep with her?"

"I am too much of a gentleman to answer that question," Quentin replied. He had to keep some facts to himself. Despite her judgmental tendencies, Avery was a classy lady and didn't deserve to be bashed.

Dante surveyed Quentin's expression. "I just bet you did."

Quentin shrugged.

"All right, well, on to the next topic," Malik said. "What are we going to do about the King Corporation? I was thinking of having a neighborhood meeting to gear up the community. You know, get them excited."

"I think that's a great idea," Dante said.

"What do you think, Q?" Malik asked.

Quentin had been dreading this topic, but it was unavoidable. He was going to have to tell them about his new assignment.

When Quentin didn't answer right away, Malik became suspicious. "Q, I asked you what you thought."

"Um, that sounds great," Quentin said distract-edly. He was trying to figure out how he was going to spin this news, but there was no easy way around it. He was just going to have to spit it out.

"Well…?" Malik was fast becoming annoyed at Quentin's lack of response. He was depending on him to bring some of his contacts to the meeting.

Quentin took a deep breath. "Malik, there's some-thing I have to tell you." He saw the worried look Sage gave him. For some reason, she'd always been able to read him better than Malik or Dante ever could. If he was lying, she always knew. "You see…when I got back, my agent booked me an as-signment and I gave him the go-ahead, so he signed the deal on my behalf."

"And? What does this have to do with the King Corporation?"

"Yeah, Q. What's going on?" Dante asked, though he had a feeling he wasn't about to like the answer.

"The assignment is Richard King."

"Holy…" Sage uttered under her breath.

"You're joking?" Malik asked, glaring at him. Was this a cosmic joke? Surely the universe couldn't be that cruel?

"Afraid not, Malik," Quentin responded. "You have to know I had no idea who or what the assignment was or I would never have given Jason the go-ahead."

"Can't you tell Jason you've changed your mind?" Malik asked, exasperated. "He is your agent after all. He's supposed to get you out of sticky situations, especially since he's the one that created this one."

"I can't do that," Quentin said. "I wish I could, but that would be completely unprofessional. Plus, it's not his fault. I should have asked before committing myself."

"But you can betray me?" Malik asked, folding his arms across his chest.

"Malik," Sage intervened and touched his arm. "Quentin said he had no idea. It's not like he set out to hurt you."

"No, but his keeping the assignment hurts not just me, but the center. A center that supported us—" Malik pointed to the three of them "—our entire youth. But what, now that you're famous you can't help the little people?" He shook his head in dismay. "I thought better of you."

"That's not fair, Malik," Quentin said. "You know

I care about the center and I will do what I can from the sidelines."

"Fair? None of this is fair," Malik hissed at Quentin. "You know something, Q, you're nothing but a sellout!"

"Sellout!" Now Quentin was offended and stepped toward Malik. "How dare you call me that, Malik, after everything we've been through together? We're family, for God's sake."

"That's right. You've sold out to the establishment," Malik yelled at Quentin, and several patrons looked over at them.

"Malik," Dante pleaded. "You need to lower your voice. You're making a scene." He didn't want to lose the few customers he had, but Malik didn't care and continued to rage on.

"And now that you've gotten your piece of the pie, you don't care about anyone else. Well, thanks for nothing." Malik walked behind the bar, snatched his knapsack from underneath and headed to the door. "I'll handle this myself. I don't need you."

"Malik!" Dante grabbed his arm. "Don't leave like this, man. Let's just squash this."

"Dante's right." Sage came toward them. "I know you're angry, but we're all family." She looked at Malik and back at Quentin. Her eyes pleaded with them both to reconsider. "A dysfunctional one, but a family nonetheless. Don't let business come between us."

"Let him leave if he wants," Quentin said, slamming his fist on the bar. "If you think so lowly of me, Malik, then you should leave before you say something that can't be taken back."

"Are you defending him?" Malik asked Sage. "Because there's right and there's wrong and I would think you knew the difference."

Sage was taken aback at Malik's harsh tone. "Now, you listen here, Malik Williams." Sage poked him in the chest. "I'm not taking anyone's side. You're both my friends. I love you both."

"Then fine," Malik replied. "If you're not with me, you're against me." He wasn't surprised Sage would take Quentin's side. He'd always been her favorite. "And you, Dante? Where do you stand?"

Dante was furious that he was being put in this position. He looked at both his longtime friends. "I'm with Sage on this. It's his job, Malik. I'm sure Quentin will do everything in his power to help. Won't you, Q?"

"Of course I will," Quentin replied. "That goes without saying."

"Hmmm," Malik rubbed his chin. "For some reason, I don't believe you, because lo and behold, your word, Quentin Davis, is worth squat." And with that said, Malik stormed out of the bar.

"Wow!" Dante turned to Quentin and Sage. "He sure is pissed at you, Quentin."

"I know."

"Well, what are you going to do to fix this?" Sage asked, walking toward him. She was torn between a desire to smack some sense into Malik and support Quentin at the same time. "You've got to fix this, Q. We can't let discord fracture our family."

"I wish I knew, Sage," Quentin said, sagging onto a bar stool. He had the sinking feeling that he'd made a huge mistake and destroyed a long friendship for money and his reputation.

Avery didn't realize she was nervous about dinner at Quentin's loft until she felt her pulse beating at the base of her throat as the elevator made its way up to the fourth floor of Quentin's building on Friday night. It was just dinner after all, but as she knocked on the door, she couldn't will her jittery stomach to calm down. Quentin answered, looking as sexy and handsome as ever in a Sean John T-shirt and jeans. Avery's stomach somersaulted.

"Looks like you've been busy," she said, nodding to the apron wrapped around his middle.

"I've been preparing a great meal for you," Quentin said. "C'mon in." He stepped aside to allow her to enter and shut the door behind her. While Avery perused the loft, Quentin immediately went back to the kitchen to check on the tapas he'd picked up from Dante's which were warming in the oven.

Avery loved Quentin's spacious and well-lit loft. The large windows facing the street, exposed brick and ductwork, stainless-steel kitchen and state-of-the-art entertainment center made for a remarkable environment. There was a gigantic living area and kitchen on the first floor, and stairs leading to what she presumed housed the master suite on the second floor. Framed photographs of his travels abroad in Iraq, *Life* and *Time* covers, and various celebrity photographs lined the walls. It was no secret that Quentin had talent, and the photographs and awards were a testament to his amazing eye.

"What made you choose photography?" Avery asked when she finally made her way to the kitchen. She found him opening a bottle of Riesling.

"I hope you like white," Quentin said, twisting open the cork, "because it will go perfectly with our fish." He poured generously and handed her a glass.

"White's fine," Avery said, accepting the wineglass.

"I had a great teacher," Quentin finally answered her question. "Someone kind and patient, who took a knucklehead like me under his wing. Mr. Webster taught me not only the mechanics of cameras, but what to look for."

Avery smiled. "Sounds like he was a good influence."

"More than that," Quentin said seriously. "He was a father figure." He watched her with a critical squint. Avery Roberts was a beautiful woman who clearly had no idea just how beautiful she was. She didn't dress sexily to show off her assets even though she had the figure for it. Instead, she dressed conservatively, albeit in the best designer fashion, as she did tonight. She wore a white tunic tied at the waist and navy-blue ankle pants. She was like a butterfly that was still trapped in the cocoon and needed to be let loose so she could be free and fly. Quentin wanted to be the person to release her of her inhibitions. There was a sexual being lying dormant underneath that smooth, polished exterior and carefully applied makeup. And Quentin intended to find her. But first, he would feed her and allow her to get comfortable before making his move.

He pulled a cookie sheet out of the oven filled with tapas and placed it on a rack to cool.

"Mmm, that smells delicious." Avery's mouth watered after she saw the decadent little bites. "Did you make those?"

"Afraid not. They're from my friend Dante's tapas bar."

"A tapas bar. That's a unique idea. Can I try one?" Avery leaned over the breakfast bar.

"Sure, but be careful, they're hot," Quentin said. He watched Avery take a delicate *amuse bouche* in her mouth and savor the flavor. He was immediately aroused at the sight of her eating, and the way her tongue flicked out to lick her lips was completely erotic. He could feel his manhood straining against the jeans he wore. It was a good thing he was standing behind the bar and she couldn't see how hard he was.

"Wow!" Avery said. "If dinner is as good as that, then I am in for a feast."

"You most certainly are," Quentin groaned.

Conversation was stimulating throughout the entire meal of lemon-dill salmon, Parmesan mashed potatoes and roasted asparagus that Quentin prepared. Avery was rather surprised by his prowess in the kitchen, but thoroughly enjoyed every bite. And she let him know as much. "I hate to say it because I wouldn't want to give you a big head," she commented once they were seated on his leather sectional enjoying a cappuccino and tiramisu, "but dinner was wonderful."

"I'm glad you enjoyed it," Quentin rasped huskily. "You'll enjoy dessert even more."

Avery put her fork down and set her saucer on the coffee table. Was he coming on to her? Because she'd heard a distinct sexual overtone in Quentin's statement and when she turned to him, she wished she hadn't. Those dark eyes of his were resting firmly on her and the intensity of his concentrated gaze made her tremble. He looked like a tiger ready to pounce and Avery had the feeling she was his prey. When he reached over and pulled one of the pins out of her hair, and then the other, she balked.

"What are you doing?" she cried, trying to keep her hair in place, but it was no use.

"That's better." Quentin grinned at his handiwork. Now her glorious mane of hair had fallen generously to her shoulders. He'd been dying to do that since the first time they'd met. Avery was much too reserved for her own good.

"Why did you do that?" she said, running her fingers through her disorderly mane.

"You should wear your hair like that more often."

"Really?" She always wore her hair up. She felt she appeared more professional that way. She didn't want to be the type of woman who played on her looks.

When Quentin saw the sour expression on her face, he realized he'd skipped a beat. "Listen, there's nothing wrong with wearing your hair up, just not all the time. You need to let loose, Avery," he said. "And I'm just the person to help you do it."

Quentin walked over to his entertainment center and flicked on his CD player, and immediately some up-tempo tunes flooded the air. Next, he opened a drawer and pulled out something, which Avery couldn't see from behind his back. She was shocked when he returned with a game of Twister.

"Are you serious?" she asked. Twister was a child's game.

"Yes, I am," Quentin replied, opening the box and pulling out the mat and spinner. "C'mon." He motioned for her to join him. "You'll see. It'll be a lot of fun." When she didn't move, he rushed over and pulled her off the couch toward the mat.

"You're crazy!" Avery couldn't resist laughing at his spontaneity. He continued to challenge her to venture outside her comfort zone.

"Yeah, I am, but I have a feeling you like it."

She didn't reply to his knowing comment; instead she said, "Spin the wheel."

Twenty minutes later, they were all tied up in a mess of limbs and arms. Somehow Quentin had maneuvered himself to be directly underneath her, while Avery had one hand over his head and her leg between his thighs. How had she found herself in such a compromising position? Quentin didn't make it any better because he was smiling up at her as if he knew something she didn't. He couldn't know she shared his attraction, could he?

When her hand needed to go underneath him, Avery lost her balance and so did Quentin, causing them both to tumble on the floor with her on top. Avery kept her head low, staring down at his Adam's apple, afraid to look at him.

Quentin tried to remain still to see what Avery would do next, but he just couldn't stop himself, he *had* to touch her. He slid his hands through her hair and brought her toward him until their faces were inches apart.

His gaze was fixed on her for what seemed like an eternity before he finally kissed her fiercely and passionately. When he trailed his hands down over her body, smoothly and deliberately, Avery could feel her breasts firming and rising; she didn't know why until he rubbed the tip of his thumb over her nipple and she realized they ached for his touch.

"Oh, yes," Avery moaned her pleasure as each second built with intensity. And as the kiss deepened, he boldly parted her legs, propelling her closer to him so she could feel the hard jut of his erection. She whimpered with raw delight as a familiar heaviness took over the lower part of her body.

His lips brushed her brow, eyelids and cheekbone before coming back to her lips. His tongue thrust deep inside, exploring every inch of her mouth, and as he suckled her tongue relentlessly, his hands shaped and caressed her slender bottom.

Before Avery could even register what was happening, he was attacking the buttons on her shirt with furor and then she felt his warm hands sliding behind her back to unsnap her bra. After Quentin relieved her of her shirt and bra, he tossed them aside as if they were nothing but an inconvenience. Seconds later his hot, wet tongue was fastening onto her naked breast, sending shock waves right through Avery. His teeth tugged at the dark nipple, bringing it to a ripe peak, while his hand cupped and caressed her other breast. She moaned her pleasure as he took her to new heights.

When Quentin gruffly said, "Let's take this to the bedroom," it was as if he'd splashed cold water on her face and woken her out of a haze. Avery realized although she desired him greatly, she wasn't ready to take their relationship to the next level. At least not yet.

"Quentin, no." She pulled out of his embrace and sat up on the floor. She turned her back to him, embarrassed that she'd let things get this far. She'd been so caught up in the moment, in the passion he'd brought out in her that it scared the living daylights out of her.

"Why not? What's wrong?" Quentin asked, slowly sitting up. He'd thought everything was going rather well. He'd finally released the inner sexy beast in Avery and she'd responded to him with the same ardor as the first time he'd kissed her. It hadn't just thrilled him, it had turned him on and he had a hard-on to prove it.

"Quentin, this is wrong." Avery reached across the floor for her discarded blouse and bra.

"How can it be wrong when it feels so right?" he asked. "I wasn't alone, I felt you responding to me."

"B-because," Avery stammered as she tried unsuccessfully to snap on her bra. "This isn't me. I'm not some sex-crazed teenager."

Quentin scooted over and fastened her bra in place for her. "Is that what you think we were?" he asked, peering into her green eyes. "Because I strongly disagree. We were two grown adults acting on an attraction."

Avery slid one arm into her blouse and then the

other. She was mortified by her scandalous behavior. What must he think of *me?* So she tried to clear the air. "I don't have casual sex."

"I am not asking you to have casual sex," Quentin said. "I just want you to allow yourself to let go. Do you have to be in control all the time?"

Those were the words Avery remembered during the cab ride from Quentin's loft. Why was it so hard for her to let go? She'd wanted Quentin as much as he wanted her. So why had she run like a scared schoolgirl back to her apartment? She was a grown woman after all and shouldn't have been afraid of going after what she wanted. When had she become so scared of taking risks? Avery vowed that if the opportunity presented itself with Quentin again, she would not be so quick to run away. Instead, she would take all he had to offer and then some.

Chapter 8

Although Quentin had enjoyed Avery's company the night before, he had more pressing business to attend to and that was making up with his longtime friend, but Malik would not return any of his calls.

"Any luck?" Sage asked the next day when she met Quentin at Dante's for a quick brunch because she had to get back to work and clock in more hours. They pretty much had the place to themselves because the lunch crowd hadn't descended.

"No," Quentin said forlornly. "Malik won't return any of my calls. Do you guys have any suggestions?" He looked back and forth between Sage and Dante. He felt terrible that he was at odds with Malik.

"I'm afraid not," Dante replied. "When I asked him to join us to clear the air, he declined." He shook his head. "Malik is really blowing this way out of proportion."

"He's acting like a child is what he's doing," Sage added. She didn't appreciate him putting her and Dante in the middle. "He wants us to take sides and I just won't do that." Quentin would never have taken the assignment had he known who the client was. Malik should respect Quentin's career just as he expected Quentin to respect the center. Sage knew what it was like to try to fight for the respect you deserved. She did it every day at the law firm, and she wouldn't let anything or anyone jeopardize that either. Sage knew about that kind of passion because they'd come so far from their humble beginnings.

"I appreciate your support," Quentin said, "but I don't want it at the expense of your relationship with Malik."

"No, Quentin," Sage said, swiveling around on her bar stool to face him. "I will not be railroaded. I know what it's like to have to put your career first."

Quentin was disappointed. "So that's what you think I'm doing? Putting my career above my friendship with Malik?"

"That's not what she's saying," Dante interrupted. "She's saying that she understands that your career is dependent upon your professionalism."

"Exactly. It wasn't like you did this on purpose

and that's what Malik is failing to see. He's being really pigheaded." Sage was furious with him. She'd called him half a dozen times and he'd refused her calls, too.

"Yeah, but you know Malik…" Quentin said. His voice trailed off as he stared down at his glass. Ever since they'd been teenagers, Quentin had known Malik to have anger issues. Malik had been abused as a child, and now he was trying to make up for all the wrongs against him by helping other people and children in need. That was why he took it as a personal affront that Quentin wouldn't help the center. "I should just tell Jason that they need to find another photographer."

"And what will that do to the career you've spent years to build?" Sage asked. "You know as well as I do that you're hot right now. You've got to ride this wave until it ends, which hopefully it won't. Or do you want to go back to being poor?"

Quentin remembered all too well what it was like growing up with nothing except the hand-me-downs he'd been given to wear from Goodwill. "No, I don't. But he's family!" Quentin rubbed his bald head. He was torn between a fierce need to survive at all costs and doing the right thing for a friend who was like a brother to him.

"I understand and eventually he'll get over it." Sage was adamant.

"You do remember what happened that time Tiffany asked me to the spring dance even though

Malik had a thing for her?" Dante piped in. "Malik wouldn't talk to me for weeks."

"And *eventually*," Sage emphasized, "he got over it."

"I appreciate all of your advice," Quentin said, "and I'll do it your way and give Malik a little time to cool off, and if that doesn't work I'm going to go see him and squash this myself."

"Whew!" Dante wiped his brow. "I'm glad that's over. Now I can get back to the kitchen and get ready for lunch."

"So, now that Dante's gone," Sage said, "let's get down to basics. What's up with you and the art-gallery woman? How's the bet going?"

Quentin thought about it for a moment. Avery Roberts had become more real to him than just some bet. She was a vibrant woman and one he wanted tremendously. "Everything is going just fine."

Sage peered into Quentin's dark brown eyes. "Are you holding out on me, Quentin Davis?"

"Of course not, Sage," he said, sipping on his iced tea. He could be honest with Sage and tell her what was on his mind without fear of being razzed like with Dante or Malik. "We had a great first date at that Moroccan restaurant I took you to when I visited last year."

"Oh yeah." Sage nodded. "I remember that place. Great ambience." She recalled the beautifully decorated interior.

"It got even better when Avery belly danced for me." Quentin smiled. He couldn't forget the sway of her hips as they'd twisted and gyrated to the music. His groin even tightened in response.

"Get out! You got Ms. Priss to actually loosen up and belly dance?" Sage chuckled. "Wonders never cease!"

"I sure did *and* she rode on my motorcycle," Quentin said. "And did I mention that she came over to my loft for dinner last night?"

"And?" Sage knew there was more to the story.

"And nothing. We had a great time."

"I've got to hand it to you, Quentin. You have a way with the ladies. I'm sure she has no idea what's in store for her, does she?"

Quentin rubbed his goatee. What he had in store for Avery Roberts would not only please her but be pleasurable for the both of them. Had she not run away the other night, Quentin was sure they would have become intimate. He was curious to see what else lay beneath that cool exterior. If last night was any indication, he was in for a wonderful surprise.

"Jenna, I want to make a change," Avery said when she met up with her best friend in the foyer of the Dominic Sabatani Salon. Avery was impressed by the opulent furnishings and artistic details. The interior designer had left nothing to chance, from the floor-to-ceiling windows to the Venetian-style glass chandeliers.

"A change? What kind of change?" Jenna asked excitedly, rubbing her hands together. "Are you finally going to give me the chance to make you over?"

"Yes," Avery stated unequivocally. "It's time I change my image. You know, spice things up." After last night with Quentin, she'd thought long and hard about how closed off she'd become and had decided she needed a change.

"What brought this on?" Jenna asked.

"Well…" Avery started. "I'm not one to kiss and tell, but things between me and the photographer have heated up."

Jenna's eyes grew wide. "How heated did they get?"

"We nearly made love on the floor of his loft last night," Avery said and couldn't resist smiling.

"Nearly? Why didn't you finish? If it were me with Quentin Davis, wild horses wouldn't have been able to pull me out of his bed."

Avery shrugged and slid her fingers through her hair. "I don't know, Jenna…. Call it what you want. Fear. Propriety. Lack of confidence. I don't know. And even though I wanted him as much as he wanted me, something stopped me. And life is much too short for regrets."

"And you think a makeover is going to instantly

change that?" Jenna snapped her fingers. "It will give you self-confidence, but, my dear, the rest is up to you."

"Well, then let's get to it," Avery said, standing up from the reception bench.

"Great!" Jenna said. "What stylist did they book you with?"

"Star."

"No, no." Jenna shook her head. "That will never do." She walked over to the reception area. "Let me talk to Dominic, please. Tell him it's Jenna Chambers."

A few minutes later, Dominic Sabatani swept into the reception area and kissed both of Jenna's cheeks. "My dear, it's so good to see you."

"You, too, Dominic," Jenna said. "But my friend here—" she motioned to Avery to come over "—is in need of your help and she must, must, must be cut by your hands. I can't entrust her hair to anyone but you."

"You are too kind," Dominic said. "But I'm booked, *ma chérie*." Dominic glanced at Avery's un-flattering ponytails and bangs. "And your friend is in need of a complete makeover."

"You have always been able to squeeze in a Tate model. You just have to do this. Consider it a favor for me?" Jenna gave Dominic her biggest puppy-dog eyes.

Dominic's eyes narrowed. "All right, I'll squeeze

her in." He turned to his receptionist. "Have Sonya wash her and then I'll cut and style afterwards. But she's going to need Blair for makeup and Emily for nails to complete the look."

"You are a lifesaver, Dominic," Jenna said. "And I am in your debt."

"And one day I'm going to collect on all the favors you owe me," Dominic chuckled and then glanced down at his watch. "Get draped and after your wash come back to my chair." And just as quickly as he'd come in, he was gone.

"Sure thing," Jenna said to his retreating figure. "Prepare to say goodbye to the old you." She walked toward Avery and grabbed her by the elbow. "Because a new world awaits you."

Three hours later, Avery was stunned at the sexy woman staring back at her from the golden-leafed mirror. Dominic Sabatani had worked a miracle and transformed her former bland hair and bangs into a work of art. He'd used his shears to create a chic, razor cut, keeping most of her length, but adding volume with varying layers. Avery was very pleased with the results. Blair had applied the right shade of foundation, eye shadow and lip gloss, revealing a sultry, sexy woman with arched eyebrows that Avery hardly recognized.

"Bella," Dominic said when he stopped over on his way to receive another client.

"She does look amazing." Jenna nodded in agreement. She'd stayed with Avery throughout the makeover to be sure she achieved the right look.

"Thank you." Avery beamed.

"Come back again," Dominic replied.

"I most definitely will," she said, rising from the silk-draped stool. She took a moment to admire herself one final time before turning to Jenna. "So, are you ready for some shopping because I can't have a new hairdo without some new clothes to match."

"Go shopping, girlfriend, you don't ever need to ask," Jenna replied and together the two of them joyfully bounced right out of the salon. They finished their day with stops at Macy's and Bloomingdale's, which left Avery's wallet bare by the time she returned to her apartment with several bags tucked underneath her arm. She was nearly inside when her home phone rang. She quickly fumbled in her purse for her keys and inserted them into the lock. Once inside, she dropped her bags and made a dash for the phone.

"Hello," she said, out of breath.

"Avery, are you all right?" Quentin asked from the other end.

"Oh, I'm fine. I just came in from shopping with Jenna," she replied.

"Listen, Avery, about last night," Quentin began.

"Stop," she interrupted him. "If you were about to apologize. None is required. We both know I wanted you as much as you wanted me."

"Then what happened?"

"I don't know. I guess I froze. Can we take it from the top and see what happens next?" Avery didn't want to remember what a fool she'd been to leave his loft. If she got another chance, she wouldn't walk away.

"Yes, we can," Quentin replied. "How about a picnic on Saturday in Central Park?"

"Sounds great," Avery said, smiling through the phone. "I'll bring all the trimmings." After she hung up, she took a moment to admire herself in the hall mirror. Come Saturday, Quentin Davis would meet the new and improved Avery Roberts, one who wasn't afraid to take a risk.

Bright and early on Monday, Quentin began shadowing Richard King. His press secretary had arranged for Quentin to follow him to several important functions over the next couple of weeks, all in an effort to get Quentin to photograph King favorably as a rising entrepreneur and not a ruthless tycoon. The first of which was a weekly business meeting with his top executives to go over impending deals.

Quentin had been allowed to set up his equipment in the boardroom prior to the start of the meeting so that he'd have a good angle to shoot King. As the executives started to pile in, Quentin focused the camera lens toward the head of the table. The meeting was in full swing for several minutes before Richard finally arrived. Everyone rose from the table as if he were royalty. Quentin snapped a photograph.

The flash caused Richard to look in Quentin's direction. "Mr. Davis, I'd forgot you were going to be here. Have you been introduced?"

"No, but it's not important," Quentin replied. He liked to be in the background when he was working. Then he could capture the unexpected.

"Everyone, I'd like to introduce world-renowned photographer, Quentin Davis. Mr. Davis is going to be shooting a spread on me for *Capitalist Magazine*. Please give him your full cooperation." The executives nodded their heads.

An hour later, Quentin had several interesting shots. One of which was Richard pulling off his jacket, one of Richard rolling up his sleeves and another when he loosened his tie to get down to business. Quentin was rather surprised that he didn't let his right-hand man do all the work for him. Instead, Richard seemed apprised of all the pressing deals going on in his multimillion-dollar enterprise and wasn't afraid of getting his hands dirty. Quentin had expected a tyrant; instead he got a man who listened to his top executives' ideas and suggestions yet offered a firm hand to guide them in the right direction. Quentin couldn't help but be impressed by Richard's fairness. How could a man treat his employees fairly on one hand and destroy a community on the other? Quentin just didn't understand it.

When the conversation turned to the Harlem deal, Quentin's ears perked up. The architect was led in with a mock-up model of the proposed site that would house residential condominiums, offices, retail stores and several restaurants. It was an ambitious deal and one that apparently Richard King wanted desperately. When it came to discussion of how to convince the store owners to sell, Quentin felt it was unethical to stay. "If you'll excuse me," he said and started toward the door.

"No, stay," Richard said, rising from his seat and shutting the door. "This is a new project that the King Corporation has in development. I'm very excited about it. Please stay."

Quentin didn't want to hear of any underhanded methods they were willing to use to run poor people out of their community, but Richard had insisted, so he stayed put.

One of his top executives began. "Richard, our main opposition is the community center. That center is the lifeblood of the community. Without its support, this project is doomed."

"How do we get it?" Richard asked, rubbing his chin thoughtfully.

"The director and community-center board adamantly refuse to even hear our offer. We've proposed rebuilding the center in another location down the street. The new building would have all the latest computer and high-tech medical equipment available, but they will not budge."

"Perhaps I should go by the site myself later in the week and talk with the director," Richard said.

He remembered a time when he'd frequented Harlem in his youth. It held a lot of dear memories for him, ones he would never forget.

"Are you sure that's a good idea, Richard?" an executive asked. "I can handle this."

"I'm sure you can, but I think I'll stop by there later in the week. Quentin, you should join me and take some photographs."

Quentin hated that idea. What if Malik saw the two of them together? That would only further infuriate his dear friend.

"As you wish." The executive sat down, clearly defeated.

"Don't worry, you're still in charge of this deal," Richard said, "but before we get too far financially, I want to know we've got all the bases covered. With that being said, I have another meeting to attend to. Meeting adjourned."

Richard swiftly headed to the door, leaving Quentin to wonder just how far Richard King would go to seal this deal. And what did that mean for the community center and Malik?

When Avery came to work on Monday morning with her new haircut and wearing a black pencil skirt, cream lace halter and short black jacket, Hunter commented on her appearance.

"Avery, what did you do to yourself?" he asked, eyeing her up and down. He'd seen her look polished before, but this was different. This sexy new look stopped traffic.

"I had a little makeover at the Dominic Sabatani Salon," Avery replied, smiling confidently.

"Well, you look great," Hunter said, glancing at her, and just as soon as he'd said something nice, he took the words away with a sorry comment. "I'm sure your new look will do wonders for the gallery."

"Excuse me," Avery said, folding her arms across her chest. "Are you saying that my former appearance brought down the gallery?" She'd always dressed appropriately.

"No, of course not. Don't be so touchy." Hunter patted her shoulder. "You've always been the utmost of professionalism. I merely meant that…"

"That I wasn't all that attractive before?" Avery said. "Thanks a lot, Hunter. You really have a way with the compliments. You need to stop while you're ahead." She turned on her heel and walked away.

"I merely meant you're more appealing to a buyer now," Hunter explained to her retreating back as she stalked up the stairs to her office.

Avery could just wring that guy's neck. Everything he said was laced with venom. She was going through the mail and her paperwork when she stumbled upon the fax from Woody from the other day. Why had she left the certificate at work instead of taking it home? Perhaps because she was running away from the unknown as she had done with

Quentin on Friday night. Maybe it was time she confronted the truth head-on rather than fear it. Slowly, Avery slid the cover sheet off to reveal her Certificate of Live Birth. She learned she was named Baby Gordon. Had her birth mother been too busy to give her a name? She was born at 1:54 p.m. on November 3, 1974, in Manchester, New Hampshire, to Leah Gordon. But what Woody hadn't revealed over the phone was that her birth father's name had been left blank. Had her birth mother not known who her father was? Or had she been so ashamed at having a child out of wedlock that she'd left his name off on purpose?

The certificate claimed her mother's birthplace was Manchester and listed an address, but was that the truth? Had her birth mother given a fake address and birthplace so that she'd never be found? It was the first time Avery thought that maybe she wouldn't want to be found. But why not? How could a mother not want to know the child she gave away was all right? Had lived a good life? Her birth mother would want to meet her, Avery convinced herself. She was positive of it and when Woody found her, they would take steps to form some kind of relationship. Avery wasn't sure what that would be, but she would not expect the worst. Instead, she would hope for the best.

Malik had had a couple of days to cool off when Quentin stopped by the community center for his

Monday afternoon photography session with the boys. When he arrived, he found that the room Malik had promised was being used.

Furious, Quentin stormed into Malik's office. He was in a meeting and sitting at a circular table with several people when Quentin burst in. "Malik, I want to talk to you *now!*"

Malik glanced in Quentin's direction and turned to his colleagues. "If you'll all excuse me, I'd like to talk to Mr. Davis," he said. They rose from their chairs and quickly exited the room.

"Quentin, don't come in here starting trouble because that's the last thing I need right now. Why don't you just go back to your SoHo loft or Rome or Paris or wherever you feel comfortable these days and leave me to deal with real life issues?"

"Malik." Quentin walked up to his best friend and looked him dead in the eye. "I know you may be upset with me, but that is no reason for you to take it out on those boys. I gave them my word."

"Your word," Malik laughed derisively. "Your word isn't worth squat. I believe you gave *me* your word that you would help the center and as soon as it wasn't convenient for you or it might interfere with your next big paycheck, you bailed. Leaving me holding the bag. Well, you know what, Q? I won't let you do that to those young men."

"*I* am not doing anything to them." Quentin's voice rose. "You're the one that's punishing them. I know they enjoyed that lesson and I was eager to see what they'd come up with."

"Well, don't bother," Malik said. "We don't need you. Andrew was kind enough to volunteer and take your place. Since unlike you, he cares about this center."

"That's not fair, Malik." Quentin shook his head. "I want to be here and I would think that would be obvious by the generous donation I gave last week."

"Money? Sure, we could use that anytime. But what we needed from you was clout and influence and since you can't be bothered, then consider your services no longer needed." Malik reached into his desk, pulled out the check Quentin had signed and held it out to him. "Here, take it. We don't need your guilt money either."

Quentin was crushed. "Keep it." He shook his head. "Whether you approve of my actions or not, the center needs it." He started toward the door, but then stopped. "I'm really sorry you feel this way, Malik. I came here today to try and make amends. We've been friends for a long time. Hell, you've been a brother to me when I had no one. You and Dante have gotten me out of more scrapes than I can remember. But if this is the way you want it, then I'll honor your wishes and stay away."

"I would appreciate that," Malik replied and turned his back on Quentin. "Now could you please close the door on your way out?"

Quietly, Quentin shut the door behind himself and walked out of the center, and perhaps out of Malik's life for good.

Chapter 9

There wasn't a cloud in the sky on Saturday when Avery and Quentin met for a picnic on the Great Lawn in the middle of Central Park. The green grass, colorful trees and blooming flowers was a romantic setting for their third date. Quentin had dressed casually for the occasion in a Tommy Bahama shirt and linen trousers while he waited by the Bethesda Fountain. He was snapping photos when a stylish woman walked toward him and kissed him on the cheek.

"Avery?" Quentin's gaze traveled up and down her slender frame, from her skinny capris that showed off her narrow waist to her skimpy halter tank underneath a shrug that revealed a generous swell of breasts. She sure didn't look like the Avery Roberts he knew. Sheer foundation adorned her face and mascara and shadow tinted her eyes, but once she smiled back at him and he made contact with those brilliant green eyes of hers, Quentin knew she was one and the same. "Wow!" He drew a shallow breath.

"So, do you like?" Avery asked, spinning around so Quentin could get a full view of the new and improved Avery Roberts, complete with new haircut, makeup and a brand new wardrobe thanks to Jenna.

Quentin grinned. "Yes, of course. You're stunning!"

Avery couldn't help but grin from ear to ear because that was the exact response she'd been looking for. "Thank you."

"What prompted the change?" Quentin asked. He wasn't sure what to make of this new Avery. He'd looked forward to exploring a different side of her, but the Avery standing in front of him looked very sure of herself. Perhaps she wouldn't need coaxing at all.

"You did," Avery answered honestly. "You asked me to loosen up and let myself go, and this is it." She placed her hands on her hips.

"Well, you definitely know how to let go," Quentin said, taking the picnic basket from her. They strolled through the mall underneath the green canopy of overhanging trees to the Great Lawn.

Quentin laid out the blanket he'd brought with him and sat down. He offered his hand and Avery joined him on the blanket.

The look in Quentin's eye was unmistakable. He liked the new Avery. No, make that he *wanted* the new Avery. The knowledge sent a little shiver up and down her spine. She was glad he enjoyed looking at her as much as she enjoyed looking at his African features and strong jawline. She had to clench her stomach muscles tightly to curtail the sensual heat that threatened to escape should he touch her again.

"So, what did you bring?" Quentin asked, looking over her shoulder at the picnic basket.

"Oh, a little of this, a little of that." Avery smiled knowingly. She'd brought cold cuts, pasta salad, Brie, crackers, fruit and a nice bottle of wine from her favorite delicatessen to wash it all down with. "Here, pop this open." Avery handed him the bottle of white wine and bottle opener. He quickly uncorked it and leaned over to pour wine into the plastic flutes she'd brought.

Quentin's mouth watered when she laid out the appetizing spread. For the next hour, they indulged in stimulating conversation along with their picnic feast. Afterward, they both lay out and soaked in the sun's rays. Quentin was amazed at how comfortable he was with Avery. He felt as if he could talk to her about anything, and so he did. He used the opportu-

nity to get an unbiased opinion about his new assignment and its effect on his relationship with Malik.
"He's terribly upset with me, Avery, and I don't
know how to make it right."

Avery was ecstatic that Quentin felt he could
confide in her. It showed that their relationship was
progressing beyond the physical. "I'm sorry to hear
that," she said. "Doesn't Malik understand that it's
just an assignment? It's your career on the line."

"I'm afraid not," Quentin said, turning to face
her. "He sees that if I'm not with him, I'm against
him. Malik only sees things in black in white."

"And life is in shades of gray," Avery replied.
Boy, had she learned that. It would be so easy if she
could just hate her parents and turn her back on
them, but she couldn't. She loved them. And
although she was angry that they'd kept the truth
from her, she knew that deep down they loved her.
And that was what she told Quentin. "I know he's
angry with you now, but he still loves you, Quentin,"
Avery said, stroking his cheek lightly with her hand.

That tiny but tender action warmed Quentin's heart
and caused him to reach over, pull her toward him and
brush his lips across hers. She tasted of strawberries,
ripe and sweet. "You taste so good," Quentin groaned.

"So do you," Avery whispered and kissed him again.

"Come with me." He pulled her to her feet.
"Since you are feeling so carefree, let's take a ride
on the carousel."

"Are you for real?" Avery laughed. "The carousel is for kids."

"Who says?" Quentin asked. "You have to get in touch with your inner child."

After a leisurely walk, he was helping her on to the back of a hand-carved horse and joining her on the horse next to hers. "You are so crazy!" Avery yelled when the carousel took off.

"And you love it!" Quentin replied.

She laughed. Because he was absolutely right. She loved that about Quentin. He was fun and exciting. He kept her on her toes and she never knew what was coming next.

When the three-and-a-half-minute ride was over, they strolled over to the zoo to watch the polar bears, harbor seals, penguins and sea lions. When Quentin reached out to hold her hand, Avery didn't object. She was having the perfect date. They were admiring the sea lions when she felt a raindrop. "Did you feel that?" she asked.

"Feel what?" he asked, and then he felt it, too. Rain. Why did it have to rain when they were having such a perfect day? "C'mon, we better head out of here." He picked up the picnic basket from the floor and grabbed her hand. But before they could even make it out of the zoo, they were caught in a torrential downpour.

"Ohmigod!" Avery said as the rain ruined her brand-new haircut and soaked her clothes.

"Don't you live around here?" Quentin said, squinting at Avery through the rain.

"Yes, I live on Seventy-ninth and Central Park West."

"Great, let's go," he yelled. They quickly ran through the park and once they made it to Fifth Avenue, he hailed a cab. Luckily, a yellow taxi pulled up immediately to the curb and they hopped inside.

"Can you believe that weather?" Quentin asked. One minute it had been bright and sunny, and the next it was raining cats and dogs.

"No," Avery replied, shivering. "Look at me. I'm a mess." She glanced down at her ruined outfit. She'd been trying to make an impression and thanks to the weather her new look was ruined.

"No, you're not. You're beautiful," Quentin responded, brushing the damp hair out of his way so he could see her face. "And you're shivering." He leaned over and rubbed her shoulders to warm her up. Avery instantly heated at the touch of his big strong hands against her cool flesh. When the cab stopped in front of her building, her doorman graciously came out with an umbrella, though it would hardly do much good since they were both soaking wet.

"Thanks, Mike," she said, nodding to the doorman. An air of sexual tension permeated the ride up to her apartment. Quentin was staring at her with such naked hunger that Avery thought she would combust if he didn't touch her soon. The prolonged anticipation was almost unbearable. Thankfully, the elevator stopped and they entered the comfort of her apartment.

"I guess we should get out of these wet clothes," Avery said once Quentin had shut the door and dropped the picnic basket to the floor.

"Yeah, I think that would be a smart move," he responded, looking at her seductively. Heat flared brightly in his eyes. When Avery went to remove her shrug, Quentin said, "Here, let me help you with that."

He swiftly closed the distance between them and her hands trembled slightly when Quentin slid the shrug off her slender shoulders then leaned down to delicately brush his lips against her damp skin. Avery shuddered, but she didn't stop him. Instead she helped by throwing her arms up in the air so he could pull the wet halter off her body.

She wasn't wearing a bra, so her beautifully shaped breasts were exposed to Quentin's appreciative male gaze. "Hmmm," he groaned before voraciously claiming one luscious brown nipple. His teeth taunted it until it turned into a rocky peak. Quentin lathed it with his hot, wet tongue. Avery tasted so good and so sweet, but he wasn't nearly satisfied enough. When he was done with one breast, he feasted on the other, until she was so overwhelmed, she whimpered aloud.

"Oh, yes," Avery moaned as moisture settled in her panties. She pressed herself against him, eager for fulfillment, but Quentin wanted to take his time.

He pulled away briefly to search Avery's eyes for any apprehension, and when he found none, he swept her into the circle of his arms and claimed her lips. His mouth covered hers hungrily. His kiss sent spirals of ecstasy rocketing through Avery and she returned it with reckless abandon. She wanted to be closer to him, to feel his hard body against hers. When they finally parted, Avery reached down and pulled his damp shirt out of his trousers. She looked up at him as she undid each button slowly and deliberately.

Quentin thought he was going to go mad with desire if she continued the slow pace. When she reached the final button, he ripped the shirt off and tossed it across the room. Then he swept her weightlessly into his arms and marched toward her bedroom. She was surprised he remembered since she'd only shown him once. He gently deposited her on the bed, but Avery sat up. She didn't want to be a bystander; she wanted to be an equal participant.

She threw the covers back and beckoned him with her index finger. "Come here," she ordered.

Quentin smiled. "My, my, aren't we eager?" He was enjoying this new self-confident Avery and allowed her to unzip his trousers.

"Yes, I am," she replied, pushing them down his legs. "I want you, Quentin Davis."

"Oh, you can have me, Avery. The question is, can you handle it?" he challenged, stepping out of his pants and joining her on the bed. Now it was her turn. She wasn't nearly naked enough. He reached for the zipper on her capris.

"Oh, I can handle it." She smiled seductively at him as she lifted her hips, allowing him easier access to remove her capris. When Quentin hooked his finger in her sexy bikini panties next, they followed the same path as her capris and quickly hit the floor.

Quentin gently laid her back on the bed and spread her legs. Then he brought his warm mouth in contact with that intimate part of her and hovered, leaving Avery eager for him to know her fully. When she finally felt the entry of his teasing tongue at the apex of her womanhood, she couldn't resist lifting her bottom off the bed. That was when Quentin grasped her hips firmly in his hands and tongued her, devouring her greedily. A spasm quickly engulfed Avery and a scream escaped from her lips. As she came, her womanly scent inflamed Quentin while her moans were music to his ears. He moved back upward and nuzzled the skin at the nape of her neck.

"Quentin, take me now," she whimpered as her hands restlessly moved across his chest, shoulders and back. "I want you now."

That was all the incentive Quentin needed to reach for the foil packets in his pants on the floor.

He'd decided to have some on hand after the way things had heated up after dinner at his loft.

He couldn't resist her urgent pleas and after protecting them with a condom first, only then did he shift his body over hers and slide his painfully hard erection into her moist center, her heat, her fire. He began thrusting deep inside. He wanted to possess her as no other man had. When Avery bucked underneath him, Quentin had to cup her bottom before he slipped out. He didn't want to lose one ounce of their momentum. Making love with Avery was a deeply carnal pleasure that he wanted to enjoy and enjoy. He smiled when he heard the lustful sounds of their mutual pleasure echoing off the walls.

Avery locked her fingers behind his head and branded him hers with a stirringly passionate kiss seconds before she let out a wild, unfettered cry and climaxed violently. Quentin was not slow to follow as nirvana soon overtook him. Afterward, he threw a sheet over their satiated bodies.

"Wow, that was pretty incredible," Avery said when she finally caught her breath and was able to sit upright.

"You're telling me," Quentin said. "I didn't know you'd be such a tigress." She'd given herself so completely, she'd thrown him for a loop.

"I didn't know I was capable of that kind of passion. Quite frankly, I've never cared for sex. I could take it or leave it. Other men never made me feel the way you make me feel, Quentin."

He stared down at her and gently stroked her hair. He appreciated her forthrightness. She was being so open and honest, it made him feel guilty for not doing the same. He'd bet his friends that he could get Avery into bed, and now that he'd won, he felt he'd lost something, too. Because if he ever told her about the truth, she'd never forgive him.

"You know, being with you, Quentin, has changed me. I feel more alive and open to new experiences."

"Such as…"

"I don't know." Avery shrugged and lowered her lashes. "Whatever you'd like to explore."

And that was exactly what they did for the next few hours. They took the time to explore one another's bodies and find out their likes and dislikes. Avery was even open to new positions she had never tried in her previous sexual relationships.

Afterward, following a short nap, they snuggled under the covers with the rain still beating outside. Avery was debating whether to discuss her family situation with him when he scratched her head. "Is everything okay?"

She nodded.

"Something's on your mind, though?" Quentin said intuitively. "Whatever it is, you can talk to me. I haven't forgotten what Jenna said at Blue Note— that you've had a lot to deal with lately. My shoulder is here if you want to lean on me."

"Thank you, it's just that…" Avery hesitated. "I've been under a great deal of stress."

"Try me," Quentin said, pushing several pillows backward and opening his arms to Avery. She scooted upward and into the crook of his elbow. When she did, he wrapped his arms tightly around her, letting her know it was okay to talk.

"Over a month ago, I was helping my mother clean out the attic when I stumbled upon a chest."

"What was inside?"

"Some documents I was never supposed to see." Avery turned to face him. "Quentin, I found a legal document that revealed I was adopted."

"Adopted, wow!" Quentin said. "And from your tone, I take it your parents never told you."

Avery shook her head. "I'm thirty-three years old, Quentin, and they never said a word. They kept the truth from me and the only reason I found out was because I was curious after my mother's reaction when I stumbled on the chest. They tried to explain, but how can they? My whole life has been a lie."

"I'm so sorry, Avery. This must have come as quite a shock." Quentin hugged her tighter.

"I don't understand how they could do this. They had every opportunity to tell me. Quentin, I've always known I was different. Felt it, you know, somewhere deep inside that I didn't fit in with my family, and now it all makes sense."

"Maybe they were afraid," he interjected. "Because once they didn't tell you, the lie had become so great they couldn't come back from it." He could understand how her parents felt because he felt the same way right now.

"That's no excuse," she returned. "I know this isn't a black-and-white issue, Quentin. I'm just so furious with them, I could spit nails."

"Avery, I know you're upset and you have every right to be, but your parents love you. Do you even realize how lucky you were to have been adopted? To have someone to love, care for and protect you." Quentin couldn't help but be a little annoyed that she was taking her family for granted.

"I know I've had a privileged life," she began, but he interrupted her and grabbed both sides of her face.

"You were extremely lucky, Avery. You should be thankful—some people aren't so lucky."

"I know, I know." She shook her head. "You must think I'm extremely spoiled."

"No, what I think is if you had lived a day in my shoes, you'd realize just how fortunate you truly were."

"Why? Did you have a terrible childhood?" Avery realized she'd never heard Quentin mention his family. Why had she not noticed that before? Had she really been so caught up in herself and her own troubles not to notice that he might have some of his own?

"If you count growing up in foster care from age

ten until I was legal," Quentin replied, "then the answer would be yes."

"You grew up in foster care?" Avery was shocked. That would explain why he'd never talked about his parents.

"Yes, Malik, Dante, Sage and I grew up in foster care. Because we were older, we were never adopted. So as you can see, Avery, you lucked out. A wonderful family took you in as a baby and nurtured and loved you like parents should. My friends and I weren't so lucky."

Avery felt terrible, and tears began to trickle down her cheeks. "Quentin, I'm sorry, I had no idea. And here I am going on and on about how upset I am with my family. And I have one."

He wiped away her tears with the back of his hand. "I didn't tell you this to make you cry. You're entitled to be upset. I'm not trying to take that away from you. I'm just trying to give you a little perspective."

"And I appreciate that," she smiled hesitantly, "but if you don't mind my asking, how did you end up in foster care?"

"Well…" Quentin paused, "my mother pretty much moved around from man to man, so my grandmother raised me. When she passed away from a stroke, I was put into the system."

"What about your mother? Did they even try to look for her?"

"They did, but it was as if she disappeared off the face of this earth."

"What about you? Did you ever try to find her?"

"No, I didn't," he answered honestly. "I guess I never wanted to. If she had wanted me, she would have called or come back to check on me. She never did." The anger in Quentin's voice over his mother's abandonment caused Avery to keep quiet about the search for her own biological mother. She wanted to share the news with him, but she doubted he would understand her desire to find the mother who'd given her up at birth, especially when he was coming from a place of such pain and hurt.

"Well, it looks like we both have some parental issues to work out." Avery smiled hesitantly.

"Yeah, I suppose so. I guess that's what makes this disagreement between Malik and me so profound. He's my family, Avery." Quentin's voice caught in his throat. He hated being vulnerable, but he didn't want to lose his best friend either. "Malik, Dante and Sage are all I've got."

"Not anymore," Avery said and leaned up to kiss him full on the lips. "You've got me."

"Do I now?" he asked.

"Yes." She slid closer until her pert breasts were pressed firmly against his hairless chest. "Matter of fact, you can have all of me, right here and right now."

"Hmmm," Quentin groaned. "I think I'll do just that." He flipped her over until she was pinned underneath him and proceeded to ravish her.

Chapter 10

"It was the best sex I've ever had," Avery told Jenna over lunch on Wednesday. She'd been so enraptured with Quentin over the weekend, she hadn't had a chance to call Jenna and tell her about their date. They'd spent the entire Sunday in bed.

"Hallelujah!" Jenna stood up and shouted. Several people turned to stare at her, so she quickly took her seat. "You finally slept with that gorgeous fox? Good for you, Avery."

"I'd never felt such passion," she admitted, twisting her napkin in her hand. "It was so intense." It had been much too long since she'd felt so wanted, so needed, so desired.

"So he rocked your world!"

"More than that, he turned it over on its head." Avery ran her fingers through her hair. "Quentin has reawakened me sexually, Jenna. I didn't even know my sexuality was dormant until he lit a fire under it. And I don't understand. We're polar opposites."

Jenna smiled. "And you know the old saying— opposites attract."

"I suppose so." Avery shook her head in amazement. "I just don't know where this is all headed."

"Where do you want it to lead?"

"Honestly, I don't know. We're so different. I'm reserved. He's carefree."

"But you share common interests too, right? Like art? He's a photographer, so I'm sure he appreciates it, too. Why don't you stop making excuses for why you don't want to be with him and run with it? Don't be so afraid."

"I'm not," Avery huffed. "We became lovers, didn't we?"

"And now you're trying to find a million and one reasons to end things."

Avery hated that her friend knew her so well. She was way out of her comfort zone with Quentin Davis and if she weren't careful she could fall hard for him. She'd already developed strong feelings for him as it was, and that knowledge scared her half to death. "I'm not," she lied. "I intend to enjoy Quentin for as long as the feeling's right."

Jenna shrugged. "Sure, you say that now, but I have a feeling that there's a lot you're not saying."

Avery grinned. If she only knew.

Quentin met Richard and his assistant across the street from the community center for his meeting with Malik. He didn't know why he'd agreed to drive over here with Richard. Maybe it was some warped need to show Malik that he would go through with the assignment whether he liked it or not.

"Can't you just see some high-rise condominiums here, a movie theater and some specialty eateries?" Richard's chest puffed at the idea of his latest deal. He didn't wait for Quentin's response, but instead he charged across the street and toward the center entrance. Despite his reservations, Quentin had no choice but to follow behind him.

"I'm Richard King and I'm here to see Malik Williams."

"I will let him know," the receptionist replied. Quentin couldn't help but notice the sour expression that crossed her face. She, too, must know that this man had the power to bring the center down. "Please have a seat."

A look of disdain came across Richard's face as he glanced across the room. Quentin doubted he wanted to sit down in his Gucci suit in the modest lobby with standard brown chairs that looked as if they'd been sat in one time too many. "Thanks, but I'll stand," Richard said.

Quentin folded his arms across his chest and steeled himself for Malik's reaction to his being there. Several minutes later, Malik came bursting through the door. He was about to speak when he saw Quentin standing in the corner. "What are you doing here?"

"Do you two know each other?" Richard asked, looking back and forth between the two men.

"No," Malik replied. The look of disappointment he sent Quentin's way caused him to lower his head. "I meant you."

"I believe my assistant made an appointment," Richard returned coolly. He wasn't put off by Malik's brusque tone.

"Doesn't matter," Malik responded, throwing back his dreads. "Because I have nothing to say to you, Mr. King. Trust me when I say that I'm speaking for the Children's Aid Network and the community center. They are not for sale. Not now or in the future."

"Mr. Williams, I understand your apprehension, but if you'd give me a chance to explain." Richard snapped his fingers at his assistant to hand him his portfolio. "I can explain the benefits my complex would bring to the community." He extended the portfolio to Malik, but he ignored it.

"So what are you? The Great White Hope that's

going to save the community?" Malik laughed bitterly. "I don't think so. You've got an uphill battle ahead of you, Mr. King, because we are not going to go quietly. Good day." Malik glared at Quentin one final time before storming back into the office.

Richard was stunned. No one had ever walked out on him. The director hadn't even given him a chance to go over his plans.

"I told you," his assistant said from his side.

"Yes, well, I never give up," Richard said, heading toward the door.

Quentin stayed put. He wanted to tell Malik that although he was there in a professional capacity, he was still behind the center one hundred percent, but he doubted Malik would even listen to him.

"Quentin?" Richard turned to him. "Are you coming?"

"Uh, yes," Quentin said, grabbing his photography bag off one of the chairs and following him and his assistant.

"The meeting did not go as I anticipated," Richard said once they were outside.

"Did you expect anything less," Quentin responded, turning sideways and staring at Richard. He'd come to the center since he was a child and would hate to see it demolished to make room for a multimedia complex and condominiums.

Richard spun around at Quentin's sharp tone. "I

take it you don't approve of my new development?" He'd noticed that the photographer hadn't been particularly pleased when he told him they were driving to Harlem this morning. Matter of fact, he'd made every excuse in the book not to join him.

"Approve?" Quentin asked. "I think it's a travesty to this community." He was relieved to finally get the words off his chest.

Richard didn't understand Quentin's hostility to his new development. "I'm willing to relocate the center a few blocks away."

"So that makes it okay to tear down a landmark?" Quentin asked. "That center," Quentin pointed to the building, "has been there for nearly fifty years. The community depends on it. Yet somehow your money-making trumps that?" Once he'd spoken his frustrations out loud, Quentin realized just how unprofessional he'd acted. As a photographer, he was supposed to be objective and take pictures, but this assignment hit too close to home. He'd lost all objectivity.

"Well, well," Richard chuckled. "I'm glad to see you're not a yes man and speak your mind." Richard despised cowardice. "I can appreciate that."

"Even though you don't agree with it," Quentin returned facing Richard.

Richard smiled. "No, I don't. My development will benefit the community and bring in precious revenue and jobs."

"After you've displaced all the storeowners and residents," Quentin snorted. "Sounds great."

"How do you know so much about this area?" Richard replied, eyeing him strangely.

"Because I grew up around here." Quentin didn't offer more details.

"And yet you're doing an assignment on me. When it's clear you don't approve of what I represent. Why?"

"I made a commitment and I'm honoring that."

"A man of integrity." Richard smiled. In his line of business, it was hard not to be jaded. "I don't see many of those in my world. And I appreciate your honesty, Quentin Davis." Richard extended a hand, which Quentin reluctantly shook. It was just too bad Quentin couldn't say the same about him.

Sage showed up unexpectedly at Quentin's apartment later that evening. He'd been standing near the window remembering the weekend he'd spent making love to Avery. He'd enjoyed giving her pleasure and watching her intense reaction as she came. She was wanton and sensual and just the type of woman he wanted in his bed. So why did making love to her throw him into such a panic? Because he was accustomed to being in control, but he'd gotten completely lost in her. He was struggling with the possibility that any woman could make him feel any sort of emotion, but Avery had. She'd gotten to him. Him? A man who didn't do commitments.

"What are you doing here?" Quentin asked when Sage walked in carrying a bottle of wine and a large foil package.

"I brought dinner from Dante's," she replied, holding up the container. He joined her in the kitchen and started opening cabinets to remove two plates. "Since you haven't been to the bar in over a week and haven't returned any of my calls, I thought I'd better come by and check on you."

"Yeah, well," Quentin said, shutting the cupboard door, "I thought perhaps it was better to keep a low profile. That way Malik would come by and not feel uncomfortable at my presence."

"That's very magnanimous of you," Sage said, pulling a large spoon out of the drawer underneath the counter and ladling spaghetti carbonara onto the plates. "Now open that bottle of wine. Dante whipped us up some pasta."

Sage loved being bossy, so Quentin walked over and playfully yanked the bottle away from her. "You know, you didn't have to do this, Sage." He uncorked the bottle and poured two glasses.

"I know I didn't but you've been a little too quiet all week."

"Have you ever thought there was a reason I hadn't called?" Quentin handed her a glass. Suddenly, his mind raced with illicit thoughts of how incredibly responsive Avery had been in bed and the little sounds she'd made when he'd been buried…Quentin stopped dead in his tracks. He was getting in too deep. Perhaps he should pull back before there was no turning back.

"Oh?" Sage's eyes widened. "Have you and Avery grown closer?" When Quentin remained mum, Sage got her answer. "I see. So *she's* the reason you've abandoned your friends."

"One week does not abandonment make. Avery and I are two adults who are enjoying each other's company. Is anything wrong with that?"

"Of course not," Sage replied. "But if I recall, you weren't supposed to get involved. Just get the ice diva to melt."

"Thanks, Sage." Quentin already felt guilty enough about gaining Avery's trust under false pretenses. He'd pursued her relentlessly and now what? Guilt gnawed at his insides.

"I'm not trying to make you feel bad," Sage said.

"I know, I know," he said. He hadn't been looking for anything serious either, just a little fun. But in the short time he'd known her, Avery had been real and honest with him. She'd let her guard down and opened up to him about the fact that she'd been adopted, and he'd trusted her with his rocky childhood. He couldn't remember the last time he'd trusted a woman with his feelings, but he had with Avery.

"If you didn't feel anything, I'd think something was wrong," Sage said. She walked around the counter and peered at Quentin. "But you do, so something tells me that Avery's become more to you than you'd envisioned. Am I right? Are you falling for her, Q?"

"Of course not." Quentin denied it even though deep down he knew Sage spoke the truth. "I'm not a relationship kinda guy. I don't do commitment."

She peered into his ebony eyes. "You're lying. You've developed feelings for her, but you're afraid to admit it."

"I'll admit that she's not the ice queen I originally thought she was. She's warm, kind and passionate. Extremely passionate, but that doesn't mean this is going anywhere. Matter of fact, I've won the bet, so if I wanted to, I could move on."

"But you don't want to, do you? You're going to continue seeing her, aren't you?" Quentin didn't answer. Sage patted his back. "It's okay, Q. It'll be our little secret. Enjoy Avery. You deserve all the happiness you can get."

"I didn't find any matches in New Hampshire," Woody told Avery over the phone on Thursday. "So I expanded my search to include the East Coast and I located several matches."

"That close?"

"Yes, I figured given the times back then, your biological mother probably went to Manchester to give birth to avoid controversy in her hometown."

"And?" Avery held her breath. She was sure there

was more that Woody wasn't saying and she was almost afraid to know the answer.

"I've found her, Avery."

Suddenly, all the air went out of the room and Avery grasped for her chair to avoid passing out. "You... You found her?" She pulled her chair underneath herself.

"Yes. She lives in upstate New York, in Buffalo to be exact," Woody replied. "I have an address for you, if you want to write it down."

"Give me a minute, okay? To catch my breath. This comes as quite a shock." Avery hadn't expected Woody to find her biological mother so quickly. Once she had a few minutes to compose herself, she finally asked, "What can you tell me about her?"

"Well," Woody paused. "Her name is Leah Johnson. She's married and a mother of three."

"She has more children?" Avery gasped. She had never thought about that.

"Yes, two boys and a girl."

"I see." So her birth mother had gone on to have more children. They'd had the mother Avery had been denied.

"Avery, I know this must be upsetting for you. But your mother was only twenty when she had you and wasn't ready to be a parent. She waited to have children until she was in her early thirties," Woody tried to explain.

"How old are they?" Avery inquired. "My half brothers and sisters, that is?"

"The oldest boy is twenty-one, the youngest is nineteen and your half sister is sixteen."

"And her husband?"

"A prominent surgeon. He's well respected in the community. Leah's a full-time homemaker."

Avery felt sick to her stomach. Sounded as if her biological mother had had a wonderful life after she'd given up her first child. "Thank you, Woody. I really appreciate everything you've done."

"It was my pleasure. Now if you have a pen and paper, I can give you her address and phone number."

Now that the information was right in Avery's grasp, she hesitated reaching for it.

"Avery?"

"Oh yes, go ahead." She jotted down Leah's address and phone number in Buffalo.

"Give me a call, Avery. I'd like to know how it goes."

"Sure, Woody," she said as she hung up.

When her fingers began dialing Quentin's cell phone, it surprised Avery that he was the first person she wanted to confide in despite the fact that she hadn't told him about her search. To say that she had mixed emotions about finding out the identity and location of her biological mother was the understatement of the year. "Quentin, it's Avery."

"Is something wrong?" he asked because she sounded upset.

"I need to talk to you. Are you going to be home later?" Avery sniffed.

"Whatever you need, baby. I'm here."

"Great, I'll see you after work."

Avery walked through the afternoon in a daze. She even ignored Hunter's snarky comments. She was thankful when the clock struck five and she could leave the gallery.

When Quentin slid open the door to his loft, Avery rushed into his embrace. She wrapped her arms around his neck so tightly, he could hardly breathe. "Baby, what's wrong?" he asked.

"Everything," she replied, finally releasing him. She headed to his sectional leather sofa and plopped down.

"Talk to me," Quentin said, closing the door and coming to sit beside her. "Has something happened?"

"I hired a private investigator to find my biological mother," Avery blurted out.

"I see. Why didn't you tell me before?"

"Because I thought you might be upset. You told me to be thankful for the loving parents I do have and I didn't want to appear ungrateful."

"Avery," Quentin sighed. Why did she always underestimate him? He wouldn't judge her for wanting to know her birth parents. "You're welcome to your feelings. I would never begrudge you that. My experience and your experience are totally different. I knew who my mother was. She just chose not to care. On the other hand, you have no idea who she is. If I were you, I would want to know where I came from, too."

"You would?" Avery's eyes grew wide with amazement.

"Yes, of course." Quentin smiled, stroking her cheek.

She nodded. "Well, I know now." She attempted a smile. "My private investigator found her, Quentin, and I don't know what to do. When I started this, it was more of an issue of entitlement. I had a right to know who she was, but now that it's here…" Tears welled up in her eyes. "I'm scared, Quentin. I'm not sure if I should have opened Pandora's box. She has a whole new family."

"You don't have to *do* anything with this information, Avery."

She turned sharply toward him. "Why do you say that?"

"I only meant that you can take some time and digest all of this."

"And what aren't you saying, Quentin?"

"I'm cautioning you, Avery." He scooted closer to her on the couch. "I don't want you to get hurt, baby, or be disappointed. Because as you said, she has a whole new life now. She may not want to include you."

"Or it could be the reverse?" Avery replied,

struggling to be optimistic. "She may want to get to know me."

"I would love for that to be the case for you, Avery, but what if it isn't?" He tried to be the voice of reason. He'd hate for Avery to have her hopes dashed.

She shook her head. "I don't know, Quentin." Her entire body began to shake as fearful images built in her mind. "I suppose you're right, I could get hurt, but I don't want to spend my life staring at strangers to see if someone looks like me. For once, I'd like to know where I fit in."

Quentin understood more than she knew. He remembered all too well what it felt like to be an outsider. He'd felt like one at the orphanage, but once he'd made friends with Malik, Dante and Sage, it hadn't seemed to matter as much anymore. He'd found a safe haven, a place to call home. That was what his friends were to him. They were like home.

"Come here," Quentin said, leaning back and sinking into the cushions. Avery moved closer until she was sandwiched between his big strong thighs with his solid chest as her pillow. When she rested her head on his chest, Quentin softly stroked her hair. "I'll support you in whatever you decide." He leaned down and brushed his lips against her forehead.

"Thank you." Avery looked up at him. "Because I doubt my mother's going to feel the same way. Do you know she hasn't talked to me in weeks? She was

so upset when I told her I was searching for my biological mother. Imagine how she's going to feel
when I tell her I not only found her, but I'm contem-
plating meeting her."

"I doubt she's going to take it very kindly," Quentin said.

"You're telling me. She's going to fly off the
handle. But I can't not tell her. I already accused
them of keeping secrets. How would it look if I did
the same?" She'd be a hypocrite.

"Would you come with me when I tell her?"
Avery asked. "She's got this big charity Vegas Night
with Nora Stark on Saturday night and I go every
year. If I didn't, she'd get suspicious. I figured I
could tell her after the gala."

"Are you sure you want me there?" Quentin
asked. Meeting her parents was a big deal. It meant
that they were more than just casual. And if so, how
did he feel about that?

"Only if you want to come," Avery said, sitting
forward. Perhaps she was moving too quickly and
he was feeling smothered at the idea of a commitment. They hadn't really discussed where they were
headed. "I mean, if you have other plans, I completely understand. We're not a couple or anything."

Quentin heard the anxiety in her voice and chose
his words carefully. "It's not that, Avery. I would love
to join you. I just thought you might want some
privacy to talk to your parents."

She breathed a huge sigh of relief. So he wasn't trying to blow her off? Thank God. She'd hate to think she was the only one feeling as if they shared a connection. Perhaps they were headed in the right direction after all.

Vegas Night at the Carlyle was all glitz and glamour when they arrived at the West Versailles room. It was luxuriously decorated in butter cream with Louis XIV chairs and pier tables. Only the very best for her mother, Avery thought.

But she didn't care about all the trappings of wealth, because she had Quentin by her side. Dressed in a tuxedo with a button-clip shirt, he outshone every man in the room in Avery's eyes. And he smelled even better. Strong and masculine. "Are you nervous about meeting my parents?" she asked.

"No, should I be?" His eyes clung to her green ones, analyzing her reaction.

"Maybe?" Avery shrugged. "I haven't brought a man to meet them in quite some time." She couldn't even remember the last time. It had been that long.

Quentin broke into a smile. He felt honored that Avery was proud enough to introduce him to her parents.

She found her mother and father holding court with several other prominent socialites at the doorway. Her parents smiled as she and Quentin approached.

"Thank you for coming, sweetheart." Her mother kissed either cheek and gave her shoulders a gentle squeeze. "I know we haven't been on the best of terms," she whispered in Avery's ear.

"You know I wouldn't let you down." Avery smiled back at her.

"Well, I must say—" Veronica Roberts stepped back to peruse her daughter's new haircut and dress "—you look smashing. The new haircut suits you and so does the gentleman standing next to you. And you are?" Veronica gave Quentin the once-over. She was impressed. This man was a tower and Avery didn't usually go for the alpha-male type.

"Quentin Davis." He extended his hand. "Pleasure to meet you, Mr. and Mrs. Roberts." Quentin shook Clayton Roberts's hand.

"Pleasure to meet you as well," Veronica replied before turning to Avery. "Darling, I've reserved a table for us in the center of the room."

"Thanks, Mother."

"Why don't you both grab a bite to eat," Veronica said, "because I really must mingle. It's all about raising money for the Boys and Girls Clubs of America."

"Of course." Avery kissed her cheek and watched her melt into the crowd.

The evening went smoothly, with her mother raising nearly a hundred thousand dollars for the charity, yet a cloud of apprehension hung over Avery.

Even Quentin asking her to dance and being swept up in his arms did little to alleviate her panic.

Quentin dipped his head and rasped in her ear, "It's going to be okay." He could feel her anxiety over telling her mother that she'd found her birth mother because her body was as stiff as a board.

"No, it isn't," Avery said. Her stomach was clenched so tightly she could hardly breathe. "She's not going to be happy about this."

"Was she happy when you told her you were searching for her?"

"No, but—"

Quentin interjected, "Then nothing has changed. Don't worry. This too shall pass." He tried to reassure Avery, but he doubted he was having much success because when the song ended, she rushed off to the powder room.

In the bathroom stall, tears threatened and she swallowed hard to force them back. Her mother would see her wanting to get to know Leah as a betrayal, but it wasn't like that at all. Avery just hoped she could convince her mother of that.

She didn't realize she had stayed so long inside until she exited the ladies' room and noticed people were leaving.

"Mom, I really need to talk to you," Avery said, stalking through the ballroom.

She'd kept the news inside all night, but she'd made the decision to meet Leah and now she had to live with the consequences. Her mother was wrapping things up with the caterers and event staff while her father and Quentin sat sharing an after-dinner sherry. Her father was probably in protective mode and giving Quentin the third degree. She had to strike now before she lost her nerve.

"Darling, it's really been a long evening, can't this wait until tomorrow?"

"I wish it could, Mom, but it can't," Avery replied. "Please, can we talk outside on the terrace?"

"All right, honey," her mother conceded and followed her onto the terrace. The air was warm and humid, causing Avery to feel as if she were suffocating.

"Mom, there's really no easy way to tell you this," she started.

"You've found your biological mother," Veronica stated matter-of-factly.

"I have." But how did she know?

"Call it a mother's intuition or what you will," Veronica said. "I just had a feeling. So what do you want from me, Avery?"

She stood there unsure of how to ask for what she wanted.

"Do you want my blessing?" her mother asked derisively. "Because you're not going to get it."

Avery began to speak, but her mother held up her hand. "I've had a lot of time to think over the last few weeks. Your father and I have discussed this many times and although I've come to understand why you *have* to do this, I don't think it's a good idea. Baby," her mother said, stroking her cheek, "I think this will cause you nothing but pain."

"I don't believe that," Avery replied, abruptly turning away. "Did you ever think it might bring me peace of mind?"

Her mother shrugged. "Perhaps, but I don't believe so. And despite my reservations, you're going to go through with it anyway, aren't you? You're going to confront her?"

"Yes, I am, Mother," Avery said, standing firm.

"Well, if I can't talk you out of it, then so be it." She turned and walked off the terrace.

"Mom, wait!" Avery shouted, but her mother had already made it back inside to the dining room. Avery saw her whisper something in her father's ear. When he turned and glared at Avery, she felt two feet tall—the same way she had when she'd been scolded as a child for misbehaving. Didn't they understand she *had* to do this? Avery watched Quentin shake her father's hand and her parents leave the ballroom without a backward glance at her.

On the short flight from Manhattan to Buffalo on Monday morning, Avery had some time to imagine the scenario of meeting her biological mother for the first time. Her thoughts went from highly optimistic to hopelessly negative. Because the fact of the matter was Avery had no idea how Leah Johnson would react to seeing the child she'd given up for adoption standing on her doorstep. And so Avery sat in her rent-a-car across the street from the Johnsons' residence, a five-bedroom mansion in an exclusive subdivision in Buffalo. What else could you call an estate spread out over five acres with a swimming pool and a cabana?

"I'm scared, Quentin." Avery couldn't resist calling him from her cell phone. She'd been staring at the house for over half an hour. She'd seen Leah's husband and her half sister leave for work and school, and yet Avery hadn't found the courage to walk up to the front door and face the mother who'd given her up for adoption thirty-three years ago.

"You've come a long way," Quentin said on the other end. "You can't chicken out now. You can do this, Avery. You're tough as nails. And trust me, I know because that's the woman I met who gave me hell when I crashed her art show."

Avery remembered that woman all too well. Who'd have known how important Quentin would become in her life in such a short amount of time? "Thank you, Quentin." She appreciated his support and encouragement.

"Call me later," he said.

"I will," she promised and flipped her phone shut. Taking a deep breath, she exited the car, walked across the street and up the Johnson driveway. She was sure Leah was still there because she hadn't seen her leave.

"Here goes," Avery said and rang the doorbell. It seemed like several long excruciating moments before the door swung open and Avery got her first glimpse of Leah.

Avery stared openmouthed, trying to take in all of Leah's features, from her smooth café-colored skin to her round face, pert nose and almond-shaped brown eyes. With a sophisticated auburn shoulder-length crop, slender jeans, crisp white shirt and pointy-toe shoes, Leah Johnson didn't look fifty-three at all. She didn't look as if she were a day over forty.

"May I help you?" Leah asked.

"I, uh…" Avery struggled to find the words.

"Listen, if you're trying to sell something, I'm really not interested," Leah said. "I was just on my way out." She had begun to close the door when Avery reached out and grabbed the knob.

"I'm not trying to sell you anything," she said, finding her voice. "I'm…I'm Avery Roberts. And I'm your daughter."

Chapter 11

It was Leah's turn to stare back at Avery dumb-struck. As she connected with Avery's startling green eyes and smooth café-au-lait complexion, which mirrored her own, Leah's hand went up to her mouth. "Ohmigod!" She retreated a step back.

"I know this must come as a shock." Avery began taking a step forward. She knotted her fingers together to keep them from trembling. "But…you see, I just found out I was adopted."

"I guess I always knew this day would come," Leah said, watching her warily. "But once you'd turned eighteen and no one ever came…" Her voice trailed off.

"You figured you were in the clear?" Avery inquired icily.

"Forgive my rudeness," Leah said, not answering her. "Please come in." She swung the door open. Once Avery was inside, she glanced around the mansion's impressive two-story foyer. Clearly Leah had lived a good life after giving her up.

"Would you care for some coffee?" Leah said, breaking the uncomfortable silence. "There's still some left from breakfast."

Avery nodded and followed Leah past the formal living and dining rooms, and into the impressive chestnut-inspired kitchen complete with double oven and center island. "You have a lovely home," Avery commented, sitting down at the table that overlooked a large pool. This place was straight out of *Home & Garden*, she thought.

"Thank you," Leah replied, taking a mug out of the cabinet and pouring Avery a cup from the brewer. "Cream? Sugar?" Leah asked, trying to busy herself.

"No thanks. I believe this is an occasion for black coffee," Avery responded to Leah's attempt at small talk to avoid the obvious elephant in the room. Avery watched Leah stand awkwardly by the island. "I'm sure you're wondering why I'm here."

"That's pretty obvious," Leah said, nervously glancing her way. Why did she have to look so much like him? "You want answers, I presume. You want to know why I gave you up."

"Partially."

"And the other reason?"

"The other reason is I just wanted to know who I looked like," Avery answered honestly.

Leah's mouth formed an O, and the tense lines that had marked her face relaxed. Apparently, she hadn't thought that maybe, just maybe, Avery would like to know where she came from.

Leah shrugged. "Well, now you know."

"Did you ever wonder about me?" Avery blurted out. She had to know if she'd ever crossed Leah's mind in thirty-three years, because from her stand-offishness, Avery thought not.

Leah paused before answering. "I did, but I knew I gave you to a good family where you would have a mother and a father. And at that time, I had nothing to offer you."

Avery nodded. "I see."

"I suppose now you hate me after seeing all this?" Leah swung her arms around. "You see the life that was denied you."

"Is that honestly why you think I'm here? Because I want something from you?"

"I don't know, Avery, why are you here?" Leah asked sharply, folding her arms. "Because I can't go back. I can't change the past. I made a mistake in my youth and I did the best that I could under the circumstances."

"So I was a mistake?" Avery paled at the enormity of Leah's statement. How could a woman she hardly knew cut her to the quick? Avery felt the nauseating sink of despair. Had she made a mistake in coming here?

Leah shook her head. "I didn't mean it like that."

"No, then how did you mean it?"

"Avery, listen." Leah came toward the table, pulled out a chair and sat down. "I was twenty years old when I gave you up. I wasn't ready to be a mother. I was still in college and had no means to support myself, let alone you."

"What about my biological father?" Avery asked. Because his name was suspiciously absent on her original birth certificate from New Hampshire.

"He wasn't an option," Leah returned, standing up. She didn't want to go down that road. What was in the past was the past and Leah wanted to keep it that way.

"Why not?" Avery pressed. She'd come here for answers and she was not leaving until she got them.

"Because!" Leah shouted and turned to face the pool. How could she admit that she'd been so naive?

"I have a right to know," Avery said, standing up. "You owe me that much."

Apparently that struck a chord, because Leah came back and sat down at the table. And when she did, Avery joined her. "Why don't you just take it from the top and tell me what happened." Avery reached over and patted Leah's hand to reassure her that she could speak. Leah looked up at her as if she was surprised that Avery would offer her comfort and empathy.

Disconcerted, Leah stammered and moved her hand out of Avery's grasp. "I, uh…I met your biological father at a party thrown by one of his cronies. Mind you, I had no place being there as I was under twenty-one, but I wanted to seem mature and sophisticated. So I passed by him several times hoping he'd notice me. And he did."

"And?"

"And he was a few years older than me and therefore extremely appealing to a foolish girl like me." Leah's eyes misted up. "He drove me home after the party and one thing led to another…."

"So I was the product of a one-night stand?" Avery finished.

Leah shook her head. "No, it wasn't like that. Richard and I were more than just lovers. We struck up an affair. And I thought we were headed toward marriage until I found out I was pregnant and he was engaged to another woman."

"What happened when you told him you were pregnant?"

"He offered to pay for an abortion. And I told him no way," Leah replied. "Whether you believe this or not, you were the product of love, Avery. Unfortunately, Richard felt obligated to marry the woman his father had chosen for him."

Avery was surprised that after all these years

Leah could actually defend the man who had deceived and used her.

"As much as Richard cared for me, he couldn't go against his father's wishes or he'd be cut off."

Avery was disgusted. "So he chose money over you? Over love? Over his own child?" She couldn't believe what she was hearing.

"Yes, he did. And I made the decision to have you, but when I realized I couldn't care for you, I gave you up. And I'm sorry, Avery, if I had to go back and do it all over again, I'd do nothing differently."

"So you have no regrets about giving me up? None at all?"

"Did you have a good life?" Leah asked.

"Yes."

"Parents that loved and cared for you?"

"Yes."

"Then I did the right thing. I made the right decision and did what was in your best interests. Not mine."

Avery didn't appreciate Leah's martyr routine because it didn't ring true. "Your actions were not entirely selfless, Leah. You did it for yourself, too. Because you didn't want to be tied down to a child and be a single parent. You took the easy way out."

"You have no idea what it felt like to be in my shoes," Leah retorted. "You have no idea what it was like to have to give up a child you'd carried in your womb for nine months to complete strangers, all with the belief that they would take care of her."

"But you did!" Avery shouted back at her. "You did it without a backward glance. You didn't even hold me after I was born."

Leah was shocked. "How did you know that?"

"Because my father told me you'd refused to see me," Avery cried.

"And I suppose you think I'm heartless?" Leah asked.

"Aren't you?" Avery asked, rising from her seat and coming toward her. "How could you give up your baby girl without even looking at her?" Avery's voice rose with each question. "How could you?"

"Because if I saw you, I'd never be able to give you up!" Leah yelled back at her. With how she'd felt about Richard, if she'd held Avery, the child they'd created, Leah wouldn't have been able to go through with the adoption.

Avery wished she could believe that. "And now? I'm here now…"

Leah swirled around to face Avery's tearstained face. Avery waited for Leah to open up her arms and envelop her, but she didn't. Instead she vehemently shook her head. "I'm sorry. I can't, Avery. I know this must hurt you, but I can't."

The spark of hope Avery had been keeping alive was extinguished. "Why not? I'm here now. Why can't you embrace me now?"

"I have a new life now, Avery," Leah replied. "A family. A husband. I'm not the same Leah Gordon that I was back then." She felt guilty and selfish for thinking about herself, but there it was.

Avery seethed with mounting rage. "The family you speak of is my family, too. They are my brothers and my sister."

"Who have no idea that you exist," Leah returned matter-of-factly. "You see, I never told my husband that I had another child. Do you know what this would do to my marriage? To my children?"

"Your children!" Avery shouted. "I'm your child, too. Do you have any idea what you're doing to me?"

"I'm sorry, Avery," Leah cried, turned her back and wiped away the tears with her hand. "But it can't be avoided. I am so sorry, but I can't acknowledge you. We can't have a relationship."

Avery wiped a tear from her cheek. "Fine. Fine. If that's the way you want it. Fine. But I want to know who my real father is."

"Avery, no!" Leah immediately swung back around.

"Either I leave here with his name," Avery countered, "or I will shatter this perfect little family that you've created. I want his name, Leah, and I want it now." Deep down, Avery knew she would never tell a soul, but Leah didn't know that. Avery wouldn't want her siblings to feel the kind of pain she was feeling at this very moment, this feeling of being betrayed by the people you loved most. But emotional blackmail was all she had to get the truth out of Leah.

Leah turned her back and considered her options. Her husband would most certainly leave her if he ever found out she'd had another child and had lied to him throughout the course of their marriage. He was a proud man and well respected in the community. "All right," she said, turning around. "I'll tell you."

Avery folded her arms. "I'm waiting."

"I'll tell you, Avery, but you have to know that he's a very successful businessman now and I doubt things will turn out any differently than with me."

"It doesn't matter," Avery said. "Now that you've shown me what to expect, I won't have any expectations."

Leah felt as if a knife had been stuck in her heart, but she had no choice. "His name is Richard King," she finally offered.

"Richard King?" Avery repeated the name and blinked in bafflement. Of all the names in the world, she certainly had not expected that one. The words sent her pulses spinning. How could her father be the very same man Quentin was doing a photo exposé on, the man his friends despised? The very same man who could walk away from the woman he loved and his own child, an inner voice responded.

Leah continued speaking even though Avery's mind barely registered the information. "I'm sure you've heard of him. The King Corporation is well known throughout Manhattan."

Avery nodded. She was in complete and utter shock. Richard King was her biological father? So Leah had had an affair with a Caucasian man? Well, that explained a lot. She'd always felt she must be mixed, but now she knew.

"I'm sorry, Avery," Leah continued. "I wish we could have a relationship, but given my husband's standing in the community, if this came out, it could damage his career."

"And I wouldn't want to do that. Thank you for the information." Avery slung her purse over her shoulder and headed toward the kitchen exit.

"What do you plan to do?" Leah asked, dreading Avery's answer.

Avery couldn't believe her nerve and swerved around to glare at her biological mother for what would be the only time they'd ever meet. "That isn't any of your business, now, is it?" Avery asked. She gave Leah one final withering look before storming out of her perfect life forever.

The ride to the airport and the subsequent flight home were a blur for Avery. How could she not be in a fog when Leah had chosen to abandon her for a second time and her biological father turned out to be a lying, ruthless snake like Richard King? Once she'd landed at the airport and turned her phone back on, Avery noticed that Quentin had called several times, but she couldn't talk to him right now.

She was having a hard enough time processing the news, let alone trying to explain it to another person. She was deeply hurt that Leah wouldn't acknowledge her. She had turned her back on her again. She hadn't expected a miracle or for Leah to throw her arms around her, but she hadn't thought Leah wouldn't want to have *anything* to do with her either. Leah didn't even want to touch her. Would her presence have truly been that disruptive? Avery would never know because Leah had an icebox where her heart should be.

"Quentin, is everything okay?" Dante asked when his friend kept staring at his cell phone every few minutes.

"I'm sorry, Dante," Quentin replied. "I'm just waiting for a phone call." He'd been waiting for Avery to call him back and tell him how the meeting with her biological mother went, but she hadn't called. He'd left several messages and she still hadn't responded. He was worried.

"From Avery Roberts, I presume?" Dante asked. "For someone who claimed this was only a bet, you sure have spent a lot of time with the lady." Dante wasn't blind. Quentin had fallen for the art buyer, but refused to admit it to anyone including himself.

"I suppose I have," Quentin said. "Dante, Avery has surprised me. I thought she was cold and haughty, but now that I've gotten to know her, she's the exact opposite. She's really quite warm and sincere and did I mention extremely passionate?"

"And we know how important that is to you." Dante smiled. "Seriously, though, I'm glad you've found someone to make you happy even if it did start with a bet. Did you tell her about that?"

"No, I haven't. I doubt she'd be too thrilled with me." Worse yet, Quentin was afraid that Avery would dump him on the spot. He should never have made the bet to begin with. It was a juvenile thing to do and now he was forced to live with his actions.

"You never know. Maybe she'll take it as a compliment that you wanted to get to know her," Dante said, trying to sound optimistic.

"I doubt that." Quentin shook his head. "She'd take it as an insult, because initially I did think she was all those things, but I was wrong."

"Then admit that, too," Dante suggested. "Honesty is always the best policy."

"Where did honesty get me with Malik?" Quentin hadn't seen a hair on Malik's head since the meeting with King. "It got me nowhere," he continued, answering his own question.

"You have to end this war with Malik, Quentin." Dante was tired of this feud. Growing up, they'd had fights before, but this was different. He'd never seen Malik so angry, so distant, so brooding.

"Any suggestions on how I might accomplish that?"

"Well…talking it out might help."

"He doesn't return my calls."

"Then confront him and don't let up until he stops being so stubborn," Dante said.

"Thanks for the advice." Quentin pulled his wallet out and slid a ten Dante's way for the beer. Maybe Dante was right. If he didn't let up, eventually Malik would cave in and forgive him.

"What are you doing?" Dante pushed the money back his way.

"Listen, my friend—" Quentin left the money on the bar and walked to the door "—you need all the paying customers you can get. Why don't you stop being so stubborn and take the money, ya hear?" He pointed at the cash before leaving.

"I'll do that." Dante smiled and put the money in the register.

Quentin had decided to wait to call Avery again until the next day. He'd thought about it last night and perhaps she was emotionally drained and needed some time to herself. It wasn't every day you met the mother who'd given you up for adoption.

Quentin focused his energies that morning on his last shadowing session with Richard King before the Manhattan Chamber of Commerce crowned him Businessman of the Year on Saturday night. Quentin was glad this assignment was nearing its end and he could finally repair the damage that had been done to his relationship with Malik. He just hoped it wasn't too late.

"I know you'll be working in an official capacity, Quentin, but will you be bringing a date to the gala?" Richard inquired after his meeting had ended.

"I hadn't really thought about it," Quentin replied. He was there to do a job, not socialize. He'd done the honorable thing and abided by the commitment his agent had made for him. He didn't want to spend more time with Richard King, because try as he might he was finding it hard not to like the guy.

"You should bring a date," Richard returned. "You can sit at my table with me and my wife, Cindy."

"That really isn't necessary."

"I insist." Richard was not a person to take no for an answer. He was used to getting what he wanted and for some reason this photographer had intrigued him. It was clear he didn't want to be here, so why did he stay? Why had he kept this assignment even though it was obvious Richard stood for everything he was against? The question had puzzled Richard the last couple of weeks and he was dying to know the answer. Perhaps his date might shed some light on the man.

"All right. I'll ask her and if she doesn't have any plans, we'll be there."

"Fair enough. I look forward to meeting the lovely lady." Richard held out his hand to Quentin. For a moment, Quentin thought about not shaking it, but always the professional, he accepted Richard's proffered hand.

"I'll see you Saturday night," Richard said. He strutted out of the room with his adviser right behind him.

Once Richard had left, Quentin wasted no time in getting on his cell and calling Avery. His call immediately went to voice mail, which meant she had her cell phone turned off. He tried the gallery next, but the intern told him that Avery had called in sick. So Quentin tried her home phone and when her answering machine clicked on, he knew something was wrong. Avery had gone a full twenty-four hours without telephoning him and now she hadn't gone to work. And for her to take a day off with the way Hunter had been riding her left Quentin concerned. Had something happened to her in Buffalo? He quickly packed up his belongings and exited the building.

Outside, he hailed a taxi and had him drive straight to Avery's apartment. "Put your foot on it," Quentin ordered. He was anxious to find her. He shouldn't have waited. He should have listened to his instincts and checked on her yesterday. As soon as the taxi stopped, Quentin paid the fare and hopped out.

He raced past the doorman and took the stairs instead of the elevator. Despite his athletic physique, he arrived out of breath at the tenth floor and banged on Avery's door. "Avery! Avery, are you in there!"

Avery was in bed when she heard Quentin knocking on the door. At first she thought about not answering, but then he kept banging, so she had no choice but to throw off the covers, slip on her robe and head to the foyer before one of her neighbors called security.

"Quentin, go away, please," Avery said through the door. "Please just go away. I just want to be alone."

"Avery, please open up," he insisted, placing his hand on the door. He could feel her pain even from the opposite side. "I don't know what happened between you and your biological mother. But whatever happened—you can talk to me."

Avery could feel him, too, and put her hand on her side of the door. She needed him, but she couldn't let him see her this way. See her so devastated. So crushed. "I can't see you right now, Quentin. Please just go away."

"Avery, let me in or I'm going to break this door down!"

She thought about it and she had no doubt that Quentin would do exactly that if she didn't comply. "Fine!" she yelled, unlocking the deadbolt and swinging the door open. "Are you happy now?" she said, facing him with tearstained cheeks. "I just wanted to be alone. Why couldn't you give me that?"

"Because I was worried about you," Quentin returned, closing the door. And with good reason. Avery was a mess. Her hair hung flat and limp at her shoulders; her eyes were red and puffy; she was wearing a pair of pajama bottoms and a stained NYU T-shirt underneath a funky old robe. "What happened with Leah, Avery?" Instead of answering him, she turned on her heel and fled to her bedroom, flinging herself on the bed.

Determined, Quentin followed behind her and stood in the doorway. "Avery, I asked you a question. And I'm not leaving until I get an answer."

She bolted upright. "She rejected me, okay?" She cried as tears glistened on her eyelids. "You were right. She didn't want to have anything to do with me. Don't you want to say you told me so?"

"Avery, I'm so sorry," Quentin rushed over to the bed. He pulled her into his arms and smoothed her hair with his hand. "I didn't want to be right. I hoped that she would welcome you with open arms. Surely, you must know that," he said as he patted her back and tried to soothe her.

"But that didn't happen, Quentin," Avery croaked. "I don't know why I expected anything to be different thirty-three years later. I was an inconvenience. She didn't want me then and she doesn't want me now."

"What can I do?" Quentin asked, cupping her face in his hand. He wanted to ease her pain, but he didn't know how. "What can I do to make this better?"

"There's nothing you can do," Avery replied, bitterly wrenching herself out of his arms. "It is what it is. And I just have to accept that." Avery threw herself to the bed and turned away from him.

"Then I'll just stay here with you for the rest of the day and all night if I have to," Quentin returned, untying his shoelaces. He took off one shoe and then the other before joining her underneath the covers.

"You don't have to do that," Avery said over her shoulder.

"I know I don't have to." Quentin snuggled behind her until her bottom was resting firmly against him. "But you're stuck with me, so just accept it." He wrapped his arms tightly around her. He wanted her to know that despite Leah's shortcomings, Avery could count on him.

When Avery awoke the next morning, she found her bed empty. She rubbed her eyes and glanced at the clock. It read 10:00 a.m. Had she really slept that long? And when had Quentin left? He could have at least told her instead of sneaking out. Avery didn't know why she was upset. Perhaps because he'd come to mean more to her than she cared to admit? Last night, he'd been a rock. A tower of strength. He'd let her talk or cry or vent or just remain silent. She'd needed him and he'd been there for her more than any man ever had. That was why it was so upsetting to find him gone in the morning light.

"Maybe he's in the kitchen," Avery said aloud and padded to her galley kitchen. When she arrived, she found it, too, was empty. She was heartbroken.

"Great, thanks for nothing, Quentin."

Downtown, Quentin stood in front of the Robertses' Park Avenue door and rang the bell. In the dawn, he'd been struck with the best medicine to cure Avery—and she opened the door a few minutes later: her mother, Veronica Roberts.

"Hello, Mrs. Roberts." Quentin smiled. An older, more sophisticated version of Avery stared back at him. "I don't know if you remember me from Vegas Night…"

A light came into Veronica's eyes. "Oh yes, you're the gentleman that accompanied my daughter to the charity gala. How can I help you?"

"Well, it's not me you can help, Mrs. Roberts. Right now, Avery needs you."

"Why? Is something wrong?" Veronica asked. "Did something happen to my daughter?" Worry creased her forehead.

"It's more like *who* happened to your daughter," Quentin returned.

Veronica knew exactly what he meant. "Let me grab my purse."

They arrived twenty minutes later at Avery's apartment and Veronica used her key to let them in. "Avery!" she called out to her daughter.

From her bedroom, Avery heard a voice that sounded oddly familiar. It sounded like her mother, but she thought she was hearing things until she heard her name again. "Mom!" Avery rose from her bed and peeked her head outside the bedroom door.

Quentin and her mother were standing in the foyer. When she saw her, Avery ran and her mother enveloped her with open arms. "My baby," she crooned in Avery's ear.

"Mama," Avery cried, "I'm so sorry. I'm so sorry." Avery hugged her even tighter. "I should never have done it. You warned me. Please forgive me."

"It's okay, Avery. I'm here now and that's all that matters. And there's no forgiveness needed. I'm your mother and I will always love you."

When Avery looked up at Quentin with tears in her eyes and mouthed the words *thank you,* Quentin felt like the king of the world. Quietly, he stepped back and exited the apartment to give the two women some much needed bonding time.

Chapter 12

"I'm in love with him, Jenna," Avery revealed two days later when she joined her for coffee. Now that she'd faced the past and reconciled with her mother, Avery felt like a giant load had been lifted off her shoulders and she could finally breathe again. Sure, she still hadn't adjusted to the news that Richard King was her father, but that was another story entirely.

What overwhelmed her the most was just how deep her feelings for Quentin went. He'd come through for her in a real way the last few days. He'd bridged the gap between her and her mother, and they were on solid ground. Matter of fact, they were on better terms than they'd been before the adoption discovery.

"I knew it," Jenna replied. "From the moment you saw him, I felt the chemistry between the two of you."

Avery shook her head. "I admit, there was that. But it's more than sexual attraction now, Jenna. Quentin's a wonderful man. He's kind and compassionate. And caring. The way he's taken care of me the last week has been nothing short of amazing."

Jenna's eyes widened. "That good, huh?"

"Better." Avery grinned from ear to ear.

"So, what's next?" Jenna asked excitedly.

"What do you mean?"

"Well, are you two a couple now?"

Avery thought about it for a moment. Jenna asked a good question. Were they a couple? They sure hadn't discussed being in a committed relationship, but that was exactly where they were. At least she was. She wasn't seeing anyone else. And she doubted he had the time to squeeze anyone else in. They'd spent all of their spare time together, but she still wasn't sure. "Honestly, Jenna, I don't know. We've never actually discussed it."

"Has he ever said he loved you?"

Avery shook her head. "No, but I feel it. Why is it always difficult for men to express how they truly feel?" She sipped on her cappuccino.

"I don't know, girlfriend," Jenna replied. "If I had the answer to that question, I'd be a rich woman because every woman would pay dearly for the answer. But seriously, you should talk to Quentin and tell him how you feel."

"I'm scared, Jenna. What if he doesn't feel the same way? What if he's not ready for a commitment?"

"You'll never know unless you ask him."

"I'll give it some thought." Avery wasn't sure if she was willing to put her feelings on the line again after what had happened with Leah. Maybe it was better to play it safe. She'd wait for Quentin to say something first.

Later that evening, Avery joined Quentin at the tapas bar. He was finally going to introduce her to his friends. She took that as a step in the right direction. Men didn't usually invite you to meet their friends and family unless they were serious, or at least that was what she told herself when she walked inside.

She found Quentin at the bar with the attractive woman from the gallery opening and another good-looking brother she hadn't seen before.

"Avery." Quentin rose and came over to greet her. "You look beautiful as always." He loved the strapless mosaic dress with an empire waist she was wearing. It revealed a hint of cleavage, but not too much to make him jealous of other men's leering eyes. "C'mon, I want you to meet my friends." He walked her over to the bar. "Dante, Sage. I'd like you to meet Avery Roberts."

"It's a pleasure to finally meet you," Sage said,

coming forward and shaking Avery's hand. She gave Quentin a knowing wink. So, Q finally had the guts to bring her to meet them. He was definitely in love, Sage thought.

"You, too," Avery said. "I've heard a lot about you both." Avery smiled at Sage and Dante. "And Malik." She added as an afterthought.

"Well, uh…perhaps you'll be able to meet him another time," Dante replied, giving her a quick squeeze.

"I sure hope so," Avery said. "You guys are the four musketeers, right?" She looked up adoringly at Quentin.

And when she did, he noticed something he hadn't dared let himself see before. Love. Was Avery falling for him? Because the way she'd smiled up at him just now certainly indicated those feelings.

"Well, once upon a time we were," Quentin commented sadly.

"And we will be again," Dante said. "Come join us, Avery. I prepared some dishes for everyone to enjoy."

Dante had arranged a corner table for the group and it was decked out with a wide assortment of tapas. Avery's mouth watered as her eyes and nose got a feast for the senses.

Hours whizzed by as they all drank wine and ate the delectable food prepared by Dante, who'd taken the night off and allowed his sous-chef to handle the kitchen.

Avery laughed at their funny anecdotes as they reminisced about their growing pains living at the orphanage. Avery didn't have any stories to add because she was an only child herself. She couldn't help but marvel at how well they'd all turned out after such a hard childhood. Quentin was a renowned photographer, Sage a lawyer, Dante a chef and restaurateur, and even Malik was a community-center director. They had thrived despite the obstacles life had thrown at them.

It was a lesson Avery was being tested on herself. Faced with the knowledge that her biological mother didn't want to have anything to do with her was sobering to say the least. In her head, she understood why Leah had rejected her—Avery was from a wealthy family as well and her parents certainly didn't need the scandal. Imagine the gossips on Park Avenue, discussing the fact that she was the illegitimate daughter of Richard King? Her mother would die of embarrassment. Thank God, she didn't know. And Avery had no intention of telling her.

"Avery, what do you think?"

"What?" She had been daydreaming. "I'm sorry, I missed what you said."

"Sage asked if you'd seen *The Color Purple* on Broadway yet," Quentin said.

"I thought we might all get together one night for a night on the town," Sage replied, smiling at Quentin.

"I'd like that," Avery said. She'd never had many

close friends outside of Jenna and looked forward to opening her social circle to include Quentin's friends. They were good people and she told him as much later back at his loft while they lounged on his sofa.

"Tonight was really great," Avery commented. "Thank you for inviting me. I really like your friends."

"They're my family," Quentin corrected. "Without them, Avery, I don't know how I would have made it. And they liked you, too. You got their seal of approval."

"I'm glad that you had them and you weren't alone," she said, stroking his goatee. "I just wish I could have met Malik."

"Another time," Quentin said.

As they lay snuggled in each other's arms, Quentin turned to his side so he could face her. He'd avoided asking her all week because she had so much on her plate, but he was obligated to attend the Manhattan Chamber of Commerce Businessman of the Year Awards because he needed to get the final shot of Richard for his photo exposé for *Capitalist*. "What are you doing tomorrow night?"

"We didn't have any plans did we?" Avery's brow rose.

"No, but I have to go to this stupid awards gala. I don't really want to go, but I have no choice."

"Who's it for?" she queried.

Quentin rolled his eyes. "Richard King."

"Wh-who?" All the air in the room had suddenly vanished and Avery felt weak.

"Richard King. The guy I'm doing the exposé on. The reason I've ruined one of my longest friendships." Quentin's cold and harsh tone was not lost on Avery. "So, what do you think?"

"Well, when you make it sound so appealing, how can I resist?" she replied, feigning a smile. If she went to the awards dinner with Quentin, she would finally be able to see Richard King in person rather than just a photo on the Internet. After her experience with Leah, she wasn't prepared to go after him with guns blazing and reveal her existence. She'd learned her lesson the first time. Now, she would look before she leaped. "What time should I be ready?"

"Six o'clock."

"Count me in."

As she stood in front of her hall mirror for one final perusal in her asymmetrical, one-shoulder long dress with a side slit, Avery was curious about Richard King. Would it be like staring back at an image of herself? Would she look anything like him? From the picture online, she couldn't tell. She was adding a touch of lip gloss when the doorbell rang. She'd wanted to give Quentin a key, but felt that might be giving away too much of her feelings, so instead she'd remained silent.

"You look breathtaking," he said, giving her a whirl. "And might I add sexy as hell." He liked the slit and the incredible expanse of long leg it revealed. She was rocking that dress! He was going to be hard all night just thinking about taking that dress off her slender body.

"You're pretty dapper yourself." Avery enjoyed the view of him in a Joseph Abboud tuxedo with satin lapels. The jacket emphasized his broad shoulders and massive chest while the white tuxedo clip shirt accentuated his dark coloring. Quentin had brought his camera with him to take some final pictures of Richard as he accepted his award.

"Are you ready to go? I've hired a driver for tonight."

"You mean we're not going to ride on your Harley?" Avery asked, smiling as she threw her lip gloss in her beaded clutch purse.

Quentin's eyes traveled from her rhinestone-studded sandals to her hair, which despite the shorter length she'd managed to pin in a loose chignon. "Not in that dress, honey."

"I'm glad you noticed," Avery said, grabbing her wrap from the back of her sofa and heading toward the door.

"Oh, I noticed," he said, turning off the lights and closing the door behind himself.

The driver took them to the Ritz-Carlton in Battery Park where the Businessman of the Year

Awards ceremony was being held in the ballroom. When they arrived on the second floor, guests had spilled out into the foyer as they waited for the banquet to get underway. As soon as they entered, Avery scanned the room, looking for Richard King. She hardly noticed the silk wall covering, chandeliers, gold-plated chairs and linen tablecloths.

"There he is." Quentin pointed across the room to Richard, who was standing with his wife, Cindy, and several other couples. Avery's eyes flew across the room and immediately landed on Richard, and as if he knew someone was staring at him, he looked over and smiled. He motioned for Quentin to join him. "C'mon, I might as well introduce you."

"Wait a sec," Avery said, and smoothed her hair and dress down. Proudly, she took Quentin's arm and walked toward Richard King, her biological father.

"Everyone, this is world-renowned photographer Quentin Davis," Richard introduced him as they approached. "He's doing a photo spread on me for *Capitalist.*"

"Excellent," another man said, patting him on the back. "It's well deserved—you've had a great year, Richard."

"I've heard of you," Richard's wife, Cindy, came forward and shook his hand. "I'll never forget those pictures you took on 9/11."

"Thank you," Quentin replied.

"I don't believe we've met." Richard came toward

Avery. "Quentin, why don't you introduce me to the lovely lady?"

"Richard King, meet Avery Roberts." Quentin turned sideways. "Avery's an art buyer for the Henri Lawrence Gallery in SoHo."

Avery didn't know how to react when Richard brought her hand to his lips and brushed his mouth across it. "It's a pleasure to meet you, Avery."

She was at a loss for words when he looked at her and she found a pair of green eyes staring back at her.

"Avery?" Quentin whispered in her ear.

"Oh, I'm sorry." She snapped out of her haze. "It's a pleasure to meet you, too, Mr. King."

Richard seemed taken aback as well when he looked at her. "Has anyone ever told you you have the most striking pair of green eyes?" he asked.

"They're kind of like yours," Avery added, smiling back at him.

"Are you flirting with my girlfriend?" Quentin asked Richard jokingly. He wasn't so sure he liked the way Avery was staring at King. Surely she wasn't entranced by all the trappings of his success? He'd found her to be much more down-to-earth than that.

Avery turned sideways and smiled at Quentin. Had he just called her his *girlfriend?* It was funny how one word could make her feel all warm and fuzzy inside despite the fact that she was standing in front of her biological father and he was absolutely clueless about her existence.

"Of course not," Richard said, stepping back and grabbing his wife's hand. Even though something about the young woman seemed oddly familiar to Richard, he just couldn't put his finger on what it was. "I only have eyes for one woman."

"Oh, honey." Cindy King leaned over and kissed him on the cheek, then lightly wiped off the lipstick smudge with her thumb.

Over the course of dinner, several times Avery caught Richard staring at her, but then he'd look away and she would swear she'd imagined the whole thing. Perhaps she was projecting onto him her own subconscious desire for Richard to suddenly realize she was his daughter.

When Avery stepped away to powder her nose with his wife, Richard took the opportunity to whisper in Quentin's ear. "Avery is a lovely young woman, Quentin. How did the two of you meet?"

"At the opening for one of her artists," Quentin returned. "Initially, she didn't care for me, but there was no denying there was something between us."

That was when it came to Richard. Avery reminded him of another time long ago, heck, another lifetime when he'd laid eyes on a beautiful woman with café-au-lait skin with whom he'd instantly fallen in love. It was a shame that life happened and he hadn't been able to fulfill his own dreams.

"Sounds like she's stolen your heart," Richard replied.

"She has," Quentin answered honestly.

"Have you told her that?"

"No, I haven't." He'd been too scared. Quentin had never told a woman he loved her.

"Don't waste too much time, my friend. Sometimes life has a way of sneaking up on you and getting in the way. You'd better grab hold of her and hang on for dear life."

Quentin turned to Richard. "Sounds like you've lost a woman before."

Richard nodded. "I did. I lost someone very dear because I was stupid and too scared to get out of my own way. Don't let the same thing happen to you." He rose from his chair and stepped away.

When Avery returned and Quentin lightly swept his lips across hers, she asked, "What was that for?"

"Do I have to have a reason to kiss you?"

"Of course not." She leaned over and brushed her lips across his. "I love your kisses." Just as much as she loved the man himself.

Shortly thereafter, the chairman of the Manhattan Chamber of Commerce came forward to the podium and announced Richard King as Businessman of the Year. Sitting there and watching him accept the award, Avery realized what a well-respected man her biological father was. She doubted he'd appreciate the scandal of an illegitimate biracial child coming forward any more than Leah or her own parents would. Even though she knew she would never say anything, she still wanted to know more about that man. That was why when Richard invited Quentin and her back to his suite for an after-dinner drink, Avery quickly accepted.

"I don't know." Quentin was tired of the monkey suit and all the polite chitchat. He wanted to unwind in bed with Avery.

"C'mon, at least join me and my wife in my suite for a nightcap," Richard said. "The penthouse suite has got a great view of the New York Harbor, the Statue of Liberty and Ellis Island."

"Sounds great," Avery said excitedly. It would give her a chance to talk to Richard and find out more about him. "Doesn't it, Quentin?"

He couldn't help but notice the way her eyes lit up when she asked him, so he had no choice but to go along. "All right, but only for one nightcap."

Nearly an hour later, one nightcap had turned into two, along with Richard and Avery on the sofa engrossed in a conversation about art. Cindy had retired because of a migraine.

"You should come to the gallery," Avery said enthusiastically. "I have some great pieces that I'm sure you'll love."

"I'd like that," Richard replied. "I'll have my assistant call you and set up a time on Monday." There was something so warm and engaging about Avery Roberts that Richard seemed powerless to stop himself even though he sensed some hostility coming his way from Quentin. His interest in Avery was not sexual, it was more paternal.

"Great."

On the other sofa, Quentin was fuming. He'd hoped to have a quick drink and then take Avery back to his place. He'd planned on stripping that dress off her body and ravishing her all night long, but his plans had been averted and he was none too pleased. What was the fascination with those two? he wondered. Avery was mesmerized by King and it bothered the hell out of him. He wanted her to only have eyes for him. Quentin stood up and looked at his watch. "Avery, it's getting kind of late."

"Oh, I'm sorry." She glanced down at her Cartier watch. "I didn't realize it was so late. I'm sorry to have kept you, Mr. King."

"Please, call me Richard."

Avery grinned. "Richard it is." She rose from the sofa and he did the same. He walked the couple to the door. "I look forward to introducing you to the gallery." Avery shook his hand.

"As do I." Richard returned the handshake and smiled at her. "Quentin." He nodded to him. "It's been a pleasure working with you. I can't wait to see your exposé."

"Richard." Quentin nodded. He breathed a sigh of relief once he and Avery were in the elevator. He turned to her. "What was that all about?"

"What do you mean?" she asked, feigning ignor-

ance. She knew Quentin wasn't pleased that her attention had been elsewhere during the evening but it
couldn't be helped. She'd just met her biological
father!

"You and Richard were hemmed up half the
night," Quentin responded.

"Were you jealous?" Avery asked, cozying up to
his side. "Because if you are—" she kissed his
jawline "—I assure you, you have nothing to worry
about. Matter of fact, I'll make it up to you." She
kissed the other side of his jaw. "All night long."

And that was exactly what she did. Avery was
brazen in bed that night as she unleashed her inner
sexy and Quentin let her. He enjoyed this unre-
strained side of her. Not that she hadn't been that
way before in bed—she was naturally expressive
and passionate—but this time was different; she was
the one in charge and he was loving every minute of
it.

She stripped him down to his briefs and pushed
him back on the king-size bed while she slowly
unzipped her dress. He watched the fabric fall in a
puddle on the floor, leaving her wearing nothing but
a skimpy thong.

He sucked in a deep breath when she slowly
pulled her thong down, leaving nothing on. She was
pure temptation. "Oh yeah, baby," Quentin groaned,
devouring her with his eyes all the while soaking in
the sweet lines of her slender body. And when she

came crawling toward him on the bed, Quentin was ready for her. He plunged his tongue deep inside her mouth and Avery opened up to him like a flower, matching his kiss with another greedy one. His shaft was straining against the confines of his briefs until she pulled them down and released him.

She leaned over him and reached inside his drawer for a condom. "Would you like me to do the honors?" she asked.

"Yes," Quentin said, never taking his eyes off her.

"But first, I have something else in store for you." Avery dipped her head and took him all the way inside her mouth.

Oh wow, was the last thought Quentin remembered as Avery teased him with her gifted mouth. When he felt himself about to lose control, he gently pushed her back onto the bed. He couldn't wait; he desperately needed to be inside her. He snatched a foil packet off the nightstand and quickly sheathed his rock-hard erection.

Then he grabbed either side of her hips and pressed forward. When the tip of his erection found its mark, he slowly eased deep inside. He felt her muscles clench and pulse around him, causing him to thrust forward. Avery encouraged him by titling her hips upward, allowing him to thrust again and again. Over and over. When he felt her body jerk as she climaxed, his orgasm came long and strong. Stronger than any he'd ever had in his life. And that was when he knew—there were no ifs, ands or buts—she was made for him. Avery had touched a part of him that he'd thought was closed off forever. He was in love with Avery Roberts.

Chapter 13

Richard King's assistant telephoned Avery on Sunday to schedule an appointment for him to come to the gallery on Monday to peruse some of their artwork for his home collection. Despite her desire to remain aloof to his existence, Avery couldn't help but be excited at the prospect of Richard coming to her domain. She'd taken special care when dressing for the day.

Thankfully she'd stashed a new outfit at Quentin's loft which consisted of some tan wide-leg pants which she teamed with a silk cami and a tapered leopard-print jacket. And with her stylish hairdo, Avery looked every bit the polished art buyer that she was. Surprisingly, Richard arrived later in the morning alone. Avery and Hunter were discussing their next exhibition when he walked in.

"Excuse me, Hunter," she said and walked toward Richard. "My appointment is here." She didn't notice the jealousy that came across Hunter's face over the fact that the wealthy businessman in the Armani suit was her client.

"Avery." Richard clasped her hands and kissed both her cheeks. He stepped back to take a look at her. "You are looking well."

She smiled. "Thank you, Richard. So, are you ready to see what my gallery has to offer?"

"Absolutely." He smiled back at her and tucked her arm in his. "Lead the way." He nodded to Hunter as Avery showed him several of the gallery's popular artists and her new find, Gabriel Thomas. Avery could feel Hunter's eyes burning a hole through the back of her head as she and Richard laughed and talked about the awards banquet.

"You know, Avery, I must say, I can't recall a time when someone has charmed me more. Quite frankly, you've put a spell on me, my dear, and I'd buy anything you suggest." Richard was frank. He couldn't put his finger on why, but she'd captivated him. He'd had his assistant research her, but he'd found nothing out of the ordinary. She came from a well-established family. So what was it?

"In that case," Avery said, moving Richard to some of the more exclusive artwork, "let me show you…" But she didn't get a chance to finish because Hunter interrupted them.

"Hello." Hunter extended his hand to Richard. "I'm Hunter Garrett, *director* of the Henri Lawrence Gallery."

Avery noted the way he said *director* as if she were nothing more than a peon. "Hunter, I have this. Thank you."

"I'm sure you do, but did you—"

"Mr. Garrett, was it?" Richard said, staring Hunter straight in the eye. "I expressly came here to see Ms. Roberts. She's a skilled curator, is she not?" Avery appreciated Richard sticking up for her.

"Well…yes, but I have many—"

"Excuse me, Mr. Garrett, let me make myself clear," Richard started. His face turned stone cold. He wasn't used to being interrupted, especially not by the likes of Hunter. "If I will be buying any artwork for the King Corporation or my home collection, it will be from Avery."

Take that, Hunter, thought Avery. Realizing he'd overstepped, Hunter nodded and scurried off upstairs to his office. Blessedly leaving Avery and Richard in peace.

"Thank you for that, Richard," she said. "He's been riding me for months now. You really put him in his place."

"I'm glad—I didn't like the way he was treating you. Matter of fact, why don't you come to the King

Corporation and I'll put you in charge of my entire art collection." Richard couldn't explain why he made the offer. He just wanted to get to know Avery better.

Avery's eyes widened in amazement. "Are you serious?" She was stunned. "That's a really generous offer."

"Yes, I'm serious. You're a smart, talented woman and someone who would be a great asset to the King Corporation," Richard said, folding his arms. "Think about it, okay?"

"I will." Avery couldn't believe how kind Richard was being. He hardly knew her.

"Good. In the meantime, I'll take those two over there." He pointed to two paintings that combined would put her way over the top in commissions this month. "And I'll take the last two pieces of your new artist's work."

"You've no idea what this means to me." Avery was overwhelmed. Her biological father believed she had talent.

Richard winked at her. "I have some idea. Now, listen, I have to get going, I have a lunch meeting. I'll have my assistant contact you for payment and delivery." He headed toward the door.

"Sounds fantastic!" Avery beamed. Once he'd gone, she let out a whoop. "Yes!" She brought her hands down to her sides. She was on her way to her office to write up the order when she found Hunter at the top of the stairs watching her.

"Looks like you've made quite the sale," Hunter commented. "Again."

"Yes, I did," Avery replied, climbing the stairs. She felt as if she were walking on air.

"How did you manage to land a big fish like Richard King? We are a small gallery, after all. First, we have Quentin Davis interested in exhibiting and now King—what gives?"

"Are you wondering what you don't have, Hunter?" Avery asked sarcastically.

"I know what it is," he said, folding his arms across his chest. "Clout. You grew up on Park Avenue. Therefore you have connections, unlike me."

"What I have, Hunter," Avery said, standing on her tiptoes and whispering in his ear, "is talent and Richard recognized it."

With that comment, she strutted past him and into her office.

Quentin was in his darkroom processing images from the last couple of months. He'd decided that black-and-white would pack the most punch and allow him the most creativity, when he came across the photos he'd taken at the community center. There were some great pictures of the young dance troupe practicing and even better ones of the young men he'd hoped to mentor taking a jump shot.

For the rest of the afternoon, he put the film

through the three-step chemical process of developer, stop bath and fixer. He was hanging them to dry when he heard a knock on the door. It was Avery.

"I see the red light is on," Avery said from the other side of the door. She'd noted the red light was flashing above the darkroom. "Can I come in?" She'd let herself in with the key Quentin had mentioned was under a potted plant outside his front door.

"Yes, you can come in," Quentin said. "I'm about finished."

"It's kind of cozy in here," Avery said, commenting on the amber-colored lighting as she closed the door. "Actually, I would say it's downright romantic." She came forward and wrapped her arms around Quentin's middle.

He felt Avery's heat on his back, felt the warmth of her breath against his neck, and it caused his temperature to rise sky high. He immediately turned around and planted a sizzling kiss on her lips. "Hmmm, I like the way you think." He circled his arms around her waist and gently pulled her toward him. He captured her mouth in his, slipped his tongue inside and began thrusting as he mimicked the actions his lower body intended to take.

It was a soul-stirring kiss that left Avery feeling light-headed as molten sensations quickly spread through her entire body. She clutched his neck and pressed her taut breasts against his rock-hard chest. She felt electrified, tantalized and extremely sexual, but they were in his workroom with a lot of chemicals, so Avery pulled back.

She noticed the look of disappointment on his face right before her gaze fell on several pictures from the community center hanging on clips. "These are really great, Quentin. Malik should really see these," Avery commented. "You never set out to hurt him, Quentin. Don't you think it's time you hang up your macho pride and make this right? Go talk to him."

"What if he doesn't listen?"

"You mean he's as bullheaded and stubborn as you?" she asked. "Then you both have that in common. You have drawn a line in the sand and neither one of you will give an inch. Is this how you honor your longtime friendship?"

Right then, Quentin realized what he had to do. Dante was right; he had to go to the center and confront Malik head-on. Quentin was not one to run from his problems. He'd let this feud go on long enough and it was time he ended it.

"All right, all right, I'll make an effort. Are you happy now?"

Avery smiled. "Yes, I am."

"Good." Quentin pulled her back into his arms so they could finish where they'd left off. Since she'd gone to work looking sexy as hell this morning, Quentin had dreamed of making love to her all afternoon.

"Don't you want to ask me how my day went?" Avery asked.

"Sure," he said, nuzzling her neck.

"Work was fantastic!" Avery pushed away from his embrace.

"That good, huh?" Quentin couldn't remember Avery describing any time spent in Hunter's company as fantastic. "How so?"

"Richard King came in and not only bought several paintings, but he put Hunter Garrett in his place," she said, grinning from ear to ear. "You should have seen it." She gestured with her hands. "Hunter tried to steal my sale and Richard told him in no uncertain terms that he would buy from me or not at all."

"Wow." Quentin rubbed his chin. "Sounds like Richard really came through for you." He just couldn't understand why.

"In a big way." Avery smiled. "He even offered me a job as a corporate buyer at the King Corporation."

"He did!"

"Yes, it was a pretty amazing offer."

"And how did you respond?"

Avery glanced in Quentin's direction. He was watching her and gauging her response, so she downplayed. "I told him I'd think about it."

"Avery, if you don't mind my asking, what is this fascination with King?" Ever since they'd met, she had seemed obsessed with the man.

"Oh, I don't know. I've certainly met powerful men before, but there's something about him…." Avery's voice trailed off. Then she thought about Quentin's comment and asked, "Why? Are you jealous?"

"Maybe a little," he answered honestly. "The way you look at him…and the way you talk about him." Did he have anything to fear? Normally, he wouldn't have thought so, especially from a fifty-five-year-old man, but maybe he was wrong.

"He doesn't even come close to you." Avery pulled him toward the darkroom's exit. Minutes later, they were falling back onto his bed as she said, "Why don't I show you who's really on my mind?"

The next day, Quentin took Dante and Avery's advice and went to the community center to make peace with Malik. He'd allowed this nonsense to go on much too long. He was determined to end it once and for all.

"Malik Williams, please," Quentin said to the hard-nosed receptionist.

"And your name, sir?"

"You don't remember me?" Quentin asked politely. "I'm a friend of Malik's. I was here photographing the center a couple of months ago."

"No, I'm sorry, I don't remember you." The older woman shook her head and gave him a piercing stare. "What's your name?"

Man, the woman didn't give an inch. She was just like that old battle-ax, Vivienne Falconer, who'd been the receptionist during his adolescence. "Quentin Davis."

She buzzed Malik and from her facial expression, it was clear he'd said he didn't want to see Quentin because she responded with "I'm sorry, he's in a meeting right now."

"He's not busy, he's just being a stubborn mule," Quentin said, pulling open the door separating the office and the lobby.

"You can't come in, sir." The woman rose from her desk and tried blocking Quentin's path, which was really quite useless considering he was over six feet to her five feet. "I told you Malik was in a meeting."

"And I told you, ma'am—" Quentin's voice rose slightly as he tried his best to remain respectful of his elders "—that I need to talk to Malik."

"Q, stop bullying my staff," Malik said from behind her.

Quentin was pleased to see him. His friend sure looked the same, he thought. The same dreads and toga, but he was wearing a frown. "We need to talk, Malik."

"Now is not a good time," he said, turning his back and walking toward his office.

"It hasn't been the right time in two months." Quentin casually sidestepped the elderly and less-quick receptionist, and followed Malik into his office. "Enough is enough, Malik. I've given you two months, which was more than enough time and space to get over this. When are you going to let this go?"

"I'm not," Malik answered, sitting behind his desk. He leaned back in his big black chair and regarded Quentin.

"So, how long do you intend on not talking to me?" Quentin asked. "You may have been used to not having me around, but it must have been awfully lonely the last two months without Dante and Sage around."

Malik threw back his dreads. "It's been just fine," he lied. Quentin was dead right. He hadn't realized just how much his family meant to him until they'd no longer been a part of his life. Over the past couple of months, there had been many times he'd wanted to reach out to them, but how could he when he'd made an utter fool of himself? He'd blown the whole affair way out of proportion. Of course he knew Quentin hadn't intentionally set out to hurt him, but it stung nonetheless. He'd just had too much pride to admit he was wrong or at the very least had overreacted.

"Sure, it has." Quentin smiled at Malik's stubbornness to admit he needed anyone. "Listen, Malik, you're like a brother to me and I'm sorry if I disappointed you, but I had to do the right thing."

"You mean what was best for your career?"

"Can you blame me?" Quentin finally asked the question that had been lodged in his throat for a long time. "You know as well as I do what it's like to do without. Can you blame me for not wanting to trash my career?"

Malik exhaled. "No, of course not." Why did Quentin have to be so logical? "I was just really counting on your help, Quentin."

"I know that, Malik, and I feel terrible. What can I do?" Quentin placed his hands on either side of Malik's desk and affixed his eyes on his best friend.

"Well…" Malik thought about it. "Can't you tell both sides of the story? You know, showcase the community center and Richard King? Readers would be able to see the consequences of his big development deals."

Quentin thought about Malik's suggestion. He'd taken some great photographs of the center. What better way to highlight their struggle than to show the services they offered the community? Quentin's mouth broke into a smile. "I think that's a great idea. I'm not sure how my agent or *Capitalist*'s editor is going to feel about it. But I can at least present the photos and give them the option."

"You would do that?" Malik asked, hopeful for the first time in months.

"Of course I would," Quentin returned. "I'll do anything I can to bridge this gap, so we can be friends again."

"Awww, Q." Malik couldn't resist Quentin's sensitive side and came forward to give him a long-overdue hug. "Are you going soft on me, man?"

"Not a chance." Quentin patted Malik's back and stepped away. "But I am happy to have you back in my life."

"So am I, so am I," Malik said.

"I don't like it," Jason told Quentin when he stopped by his office the following day. Quentin had brought the portfolio with shots of Richard in his office, at one of his construction sites in a hard hat, one of him at the awards dinner and various others all juxtaposed against a photo of him pointing to the community center and the subsequent shots of the clinic, the dancers and the boys playing basketball.

"I don't agree," Quentin replied. "Those pictures make a pretty powerful statement."

"Exactly my point," Jason said haughtily. He hated to disagree with one of his best clients, but he had a duty to do what was in his best interests, whether Quentin liked it or not. "They're negatively depicting King and that's not what you were hired to do."

"I'm delivering what they hired me for," Quentin returned. "There are always two sides to every story and I'm showing both."

"*Capitalist* wants to highlight Richard King's achievements, not show what a ruthless businessman he is. I think it's a bad idea."

"Well, I'm not asking your approval. Out of professional courtesy, I came to tell you what I was planning to do. I plan on delivering both sets of pictures."

"Despite my *professional* advice."

Quentin shrugged. He was not backing down. This was important to his friendship with Malik and, heck, that center was important to him. Sometimes in life you had to make a stand and this was one of those moments.

"This is career suicide, Quentin. You're at the top of your game. Why would you purposely sabotage yourself? Once word gets around that you're a prima donna and can't take direction, you'll be finished. Is that what you want, to end up back on the street, hustling? Because that's exactly where I found you." Jason's words were harsh, but they needed to be said. When Quentin didn't respond, Jason said, "Fine, have it your way, but don't say I didn't warn you."

Jason's ominous words stayed with Quentin throughout the course of the evening. Even when he and Avery stepped out for dinner, he couldn't shake the feeling.

"Is everything all right?" Avery asked. "You haven't been yourself tonight." She'd watched him push the food back and forth on his plate, hardly eating a bite. And Quentin loved to eat, though you could hardly tell because he kept himself in shape at the gym or with the weight machines he had in his loft. His body was lithe and trim, and gave her immense pleasure. She smiled at the thought.

"No, I had a disagreement with my agent today."

"Oh?" Avery became uneasy and fidgeted in her seat. She sure hoped Quentin wasn't jumping ship and flying off to God knows where. Wasn't that what photojournalists did? Risk their lives, all in search of the great Pulitzer Prize.

"Yeah, I told him that I had a different angle on the photo exposé on Richard King."

Avery's ears perked up. Now she was really curious. He was talking about her biological father after all, a fact she hadn't yet shared with him. "How different?" she asked cautiously, taking a sip of her wine.

"Well, I've decided to send the magazine the photos of Richard, but also some of the center. I'm hoping they'll see the story potential on this. You know, here's Richard King, a powerful businessman who's destroying a community all in the name of the all-mighty dollar."

"Quentin, how can you say that? I thought you liked Richard."

"Just because I think that overall he's an all right guy doesn't mean that I'm going to agree with everything he does. Especially when it comes to tearing down a place that's near and dear to my heart," Quentin responded. "And why is it you're defending the man? Since when did you become his biggest champion?"

"Since he came to the gallery and bought several paintings," Avery returned.

"Oh please, that was nothing but a drop in the bucket to him." Quentin didn't believe King's motives were altogether altruistic. He was probably just trying to impress Avery.

"Thanks a lot," she replied. Quentin made it sound as if her knowledge of great artwork had nothing to do with it.

She rose from her chair, so quickly it nearly fell back. Quentin had to catch it before it crashed to the floor.

"I'm going to go powder my nose." Avery threw him a glare over her shoulder as she stormed to the ladies' room to calm her frayed nerves. Once inside, she covered her mouth with her hand. Why had she reacted like that? Because Quentin wanted to prosecute Richard in the media. Not that she could blame him. He had no idea who he was or what he meant to her because she hadn't told him.

She'd kept the secret to herself not so much to protect King but to protect herself and her parents. She and her mother were finally back on track and this would derail them. Not to mention the embarrassing scandal. But what should she do now? Even though she owed Richard King nothing, she couldn't knowingly let Quentin publish those photos. Could she?

When she returned to the table, Quentin came

around to help her to her seat. "Listen—" he scooted the chair underneath her "—I'm sorry if what I said offended you. I in no way wanted to imply that Richard wouldn't recognize what a great artistic eye you have. Because you are extremely talented, Avery. And I don't even know if I've ever told you that before, but you are. I think you're amazing. No, make that incredible." Quentin smiled nervously at her. He didn't want Avery to be upset with him; she meant a great deal to him.

"Thank you," she replied. That was exactly what she needed to hear. "I think you're pretty incredible, too."

"Then, let's get out of here." Quentin threw a hundred-dollar bill down on the table to take care of the tab.

Once back at Avery's apartment, he undressed and peeled off each layer of her clothing like an onion, leaving her without a stitch on and lying naked on the bed. Quentin wanted to savor every inch of her, the way she was meant to be savored. His blood ran hot and heavy through his veins as he slipped under the cool sheets and took her in his arms. He drew her mouth to his. "Are you ready to be naughty?"

Avery answered by inching over to the middle of the bed, giving him plenty of access to have his way with her.

That was all the encouragement Quentin needed. He lazily circled over each nipple with his hot, urgent tongue. Then his lips began moving lower to her belly button where his tongue played havoc with her senses. His tongue trailed a path down the soft inner part of her thighs before moving farther south. When he lowered his head and his tongue teased her core, white-hot darts of desire flickered through Avery, causing her whole body to soar.

"Oh, yes." Her groans were deep and guttural as Quentin took her on a sensual journey.

He quickly put on the protection he'd purchased earlier and sucked in a sharp breath as he entered her. Avery's tight haven stretched to accommodate him, allowing him to push farther inside. When she wrapped her legs around him, he thrust harder and faster, going deeper until he brought them to the brink. A cry of pleasure escaped Avery's lips when she came and a shudder tore right through Quentin as they both tumbled over the edge together.

Quentin shifted his weight to his side and turned to face her. Avery was looking back at him, but this time instead of passion or satisfaction, fear was in her eyes. "What's wrong, baby?" He didn't like the look he saw in her eyes.

"Quentin, I really need to talk to you," she finally said. It was time she told Quentin about her connection to Richard King. The fact that they'd just shared another soul-stirring lovemaking session had Avery feeling extremely guilty. How could she continue to lie to the man she loved?

"Hmmm, what's going on?" He nuzzled her neck with the tip of his nose.

"It's about Richard King."

"Not again," he sighed, lifting his head and sitting upright. "What is it about this man, Avery, that has you so enraptured?"

"Quentin, there's a lot you don't know."

"So why don't you fill me in?" he asked harshly. "Because I'm getting sick and tired of your interest in this man."

"Well…" Avery rose to a seated position and pulled the sheet over her naked form. "Quentin, you see…"

"Whatever it is, just spit it out."

"When I was in Buffalo, Leah told me the identity of my birth father."

"She did?" Quentin was shocked. Before he could ask another question, he realized that Avery had kept this information to herself. "Why didn't you tell me when you got back?" The more he thought about it, the angrier he got; she'd had plenty of time to tell him the truth.

"Because I was grappling with her rejection," Avery answered. "I decided that maybe I didn't want to know and that my family didn't need the scandal."

"And then what happened?"

"And then I met him!"

"And now it suddenly matters?" Quentin's brow creased. "Why?"

"Because my biological father is Richard King."

"Richard King!"

"You heard right," Avery replied to Quentin's shocked expression.

"Wow!" Quentin fell back against the pillows and digested the information. He sure hadn't seen that one coming.

Avery turned to him. "Imagine how I felt when I learned the news. It was pretty amazing that my boyfriend just so happens to be doing an exposé on Richard King."

Quentin mulled the information over in his head. "Well, this certainly explains your fascination."

"I had no intention of telling Richard or anyone the truth," Avery replied. "I was going to take it to my grave."

"Why?"

"Because he never wanted me to begin with, because he was already engaged to Cindy even though he was having an affair with Leah. He asked Leah to get rid of me, but she couldn't."

"So she gave you up instead?"

"And after her reaction—" Avery clutched her chest "—I just couldn't take another rejection, Quentin. My heart can't handle it."

"So why bring him up now?" Quentin didn't understand. "If you have no intention of telling him, why tell me?" She could have kept the secret forever and he would have been none the wiser.

"Well…" Avery didn't know how to begin.

Although Richard King was no father to her and had no idea who she was, she still didn't want to see him hurt.

Avery's silence made Quentin think long and hard, and that was when it hit him—Avery wanted him to nix his idea of running the photos of the community center. Quentin fixed his dark eyes on her. "You don't want me to send those photos in of the community center, do you?"

Avery was afraid to look at Quentin because she'd felt a distinct chill enter the air.

"I asked you a question," he said, his fury starting to rise. How could she ask him to go against Malik again when she knew how desperately he wanted to repair their relationship? And for Richard King, of all people? He wasn't worthy of her protection; he was a big boy and could take care of himself. The community center could not.

Avery finally nodded. "Yes, I would like you not to send those pictures to *Capitalist*."

"How could you ask me to do that?" Quentin stared back at her. He couldn't believe this was the same woman he'd just made exquisite love to. Who knew him so intimately, but yet in the same breath, could ask him to betray his best friend. "You know what I've gone through with Malik."

"Because he's my father!" Avery said vehemently, defending her actions. She knew she was being unfair, but she felt justified.

"Clayton Roberts is your father," Quentin returned. He threw back the covers and started picking up the clothes he'd discarded earlier. "As you stated yourself, Richard King has no idea who you are."

"What are you doing?" Avery asked when Quentin began dressing.

"I need to get out of here," he said.

"Quentin, please don't leave like this," she said, reaching over to the bottom of the bed and pulling on her robe. She put one arm in and then the other and turned to face him. "Can't we talk about this?"

"What is there to talk about, Avery?" Quentin asked.

"I know I am asking a lot."

"Avery, you're asking more than a lot. You're asking me to choose. To choose between you and my family."

"Aren't I worth it? Or have I been nothing more than a bed warmer the last few months, Quentin?"

The furious look he bestowed on her could have melted ice. "That's a low blow, Avery."

"Is it?" she asked. "Not once have you ever mentioned where we're headed. Not once have you ever said you cared for me."

"Are you kidding me?" Quentin asked, befuddled. "I've shown you, Avery. In every way I know how. I've shown you." What more did she want? He'd been there for her after her birth mother had rejected her. He'd kicked his friends to the curb and spent all his spare time with her.

"But you've never said the words, Quentin. I want to hear you say the words."

"So, is this a test, Avery?" he asked, pulling his shirt over his head. "Are you testing me to see how deep my feelings for you run?"

"What if I am?" she said defiantly, folding her arms across her chest.

"Then I guess I just failed," Quentin said, storming out of the room.

Once he had gone, Avery collapsed onto the bed. What had she done?

Chapter 14

Avery was a wreck. She hadn't heard from Quentin since he'd stormed out of her place last night. She'd left several voice mails and text messages all morning, and still nothing. She had made a terrible mistake backing Quentin into a corner and asking him to choose between her and his family, but what choice had she had? She was trying to protect Richard.

Thanks to him, she'd had several more clients and referrals of late at the gallery. Even Hunter had to comment on how well she was doing.

"I hate to admit it," Hunter said during a discussion on an upcoming exhibit. "But despite your head being elsewhere, sales at the gallery sure haven't suffered."

"If that's your backhanded way of compliment-ing me," Avery said, "then thank you. And since the gallery is doing so well, I'd like to ask for an increase in my commission."

"Well…I don't know about all that."

Avery was not backing down. She'd waited a long time for this moment and she was in a position to push the envelope. "I've brought in most of the clien-tele to this place, but if you'd like me to take that business someplace else…" Avery shrugged.

Hunter thought about it. He couldn't afford to lose someone with Avery's talent and connections. Mr. Lawrence had expressed just the other day how happy he was with the gallery's sales.

"I'll present this to Mr. Lawrence," Hunter replied, "but I can't guarantee you anything."

Avery smiled. She had it in the bag. "Of course you can't but I'm sure you'll do your best to persuade him. Now if you'll excuse me. I have a lunch appointment." Avery rose and headed for the door. And for once, Hunter didn't ask where she was going or with whom. She had finally proved to him and Mr. Lawrence how valuable a player she really was and it felt marvelous!

"Is everything okay, Q?" Dante asked, walking toward him. Quentin had come into the bar over an hour ago, asked for a bucket of beer and sat in one of the booths looking forlorn as he chugged each and every one.

"Far from it," Quentin answered, placing an empty bottle on the table.

"Don't tell me," Dante said. "I'd know that look anywhere. You're having woman troubles."

"You're right on the money, Dante."

"What happened, if you don't mind my asking?"

"It's complicated," Quentin replied, "but suffice it to say, Avery asked me to make a choice. And either way, I lose."

"Sounds ominous."

"It is."

"Look on the bright side, you made up with Malik and now everything can go back to normal."

"Can it?"

"Of course it can. He's stopping by for dinner with Sage." Dante glanced down at his watch. "In an hour or so."

Great, Quentin thought. That was exactly what he needed. To be faced with the flipside of the coin. If he didn't send those pictures in, his friendship with Malik would end for certain, and he doubted Dante and Sage would be too happy with him either. But on the other hand, despite how angry he was with her for asking him to choose, he didn't want to lose Avery. She had become as important to him as his family. But if he went forward with those pictures, their relationship was over.

Malik and Sage appeared an hour later and it was as if the last few months hadn't happened. The four of them laughed and talked and teased each other just as they'd always done, except this time, it meant more to Quentin than he'd ever realized, because what if this was the last time they were together as a family?

"We missed you, you little pigheaded mullet," Sage said, tugging one of Malik's dreads.

"I missed you, too, kiddo." Malik kissed Sage on the forehead. "And I'm sorry that I didn't return your calls. I know you were trying to help." He'd missed her, but he had no one to blame but himself.

"Yeah, well, if I wasn't so busy trying to make partner and working crazy hours, I would have really given you a piece of my mind."

Malik had no doubt she would have. Sage was a real spitfire. "Then I'm glad I escaped your wrath."

"Just barely," she said, smiling. She glanced back and forth between the three men. She was so happy they were all back together again. She'd hated the distance between them. Sure, she had other friends and had made quite a few in college. Yet somehow none had come even close; her compass had always led her back to them. "Group hug, group hug."

"Aww, Sage." The men bemoaned her attempt at lovey-dovey.

"C'mon, give me some love," she said, opening her arms. Reluctantly, Dante, Malik and Quentin joined her in a group hug. "Now doesn't that feel better?" she asked when they separated.

"Great!" Dante said. He didn't really care for public displays of affection. He preferred to keep his feelings inside. "Who wants a drink?"

"Me!" Quentin said.

"I think you've had enough," Dante commented, popping open a beer and sliding one Malik's way. Quentin had finished the entire bucket of beer.

While Dante and Malik chatted, Sage walked up to Quentin. "Okay, what gives?" she asked, folding her arms across her chest and regarding him suspiciously. "You've been moping since we got here. What's going on?"

"Nothing."

"Bull. Try again."

Quentin laughed. Trust Sage not to take no for an answer. "Avery and I had a disagreement." Of course, it was more than a disagreement. A fight, he could deal with. This was worse.

"Is that all?" Sage chuckled. "Those happen in relationships. Oh, wait, you usually don't stick around for that." Quentin was known for dropping and running when things got too serious. He'd take a photo assignment someplace far away and hide for months on end.

"Thanks, Sage. I really appreciate your help," Quentin said, walking away.

"Hey." She touched his arm. "You know I was just kidding. I'm glad to see that you're in a relationship. It was high time you stopped kissing and running."

"Oh yeah? Well, I don't know how to deal with all of this relationship stuff, Sage. I thought I could. I thought that if you loved someone, the rest would be easy."

Sage's eyes grew wide. "What did you just say?"

Quentin's brow furrowed. "What do you mean?"

"Did you just say you loved Avery?"

"Of course not," Quentin backpedaled and shook his head. "I don't believe in that love thing."

"I know what I heard," Sage said, pointing her finger at him. "Don't be afraid to admit that you love her, Quentin. Because if you don't, you could lose her." She knew how hard it was for Quentin to let anyone in. She'd felt the same way herself.

"If this is what love feels like," he replied, "then I don't want it." He didn't like the feeling that he was not in control of his emotions. It scared the living daylights out of him.

"The heart feels what it feels," Sage said, grabbing Quentin by the arm and pulling him back toward the bar. "You can't control it."

Those words stuck with him for the duration of the evening. And somewhere between dessert and the cab ride home, he realized he didn't want to live his life without Avery in it. "You can drop me off at Seventy-ninth and Central Park West," he informed the cabbie.

"Sure thing."

When he rang Avery's doorbell it was nearly ten o'clock. He hoped he wasn't waking her. He was unprepared when she opened the door and threw her arms around his neck. "I'm so happy to see you," she said, furiously kissing him on the cheek.

He pulled back. "I'm happy to see you, too."

"Quentin…" Avery began, but he silenced her by putting his forefinger on her lips.

"I'll do it," he said. "I won't send in the pictures."

As she sat down at her desk the next day, Avery replayed the previous night's events over and over in her head. Had Quentin really come over to her apartment and told her he wouldn't send in those photos? He would tell Malik this evening after work—why postpone the inevitable? Had he really chosen her over his friendship with Malik? It should make her happy. She should be elated. So why did she feel like a frog was lodged in her throat?

"Hunter, what can I do for you?" Avery asked when she found him standing in her doorway.

"Good news!" he replied. "Mr. Lawrence has approved your requested commission increase."

"That's great!" Avery said, feigning a smile.

"Don't sound so excited," Hunter said. "I had to campaign really hard for you."

Avery doubted Hunter had had to do much campaigning, as her work spoke for itself, but if that was what he needed to feel better, she'd go along with it. "And I appreciate it," she said. "I just have a lot on my mind."

"All right, well, I'll leave you to it," he said, closing the door behind himself.

"Thank you," she said. After he'd left, she decided she needed a pick-me-up, and what better way than lunch with Jenna? She quickly dialed Jenna's office and found that she was free.

A few hours later, they were seated at a small café having salads. Avery had a chopped-steak salad and Jenna, an Asian chicken salad.

"It's good to see you," Jenna said, kissing Avery's cheek. "And the hairdo is still holding up." She touched Avery's sophisticated razor-cut style.

"Thanks," Avery said. She'd been back to Dominic Sabatini for a trim to maintain the look.

"What's wrong?" Jenna asked, putting a forkful of salad to her lips. "Last we spoke, you were in love and on cloud nine."

"I know, I know. And now I've gone and ruined it."

"What did you do?"

"I put Quentin in an untenable situation and asked him to choose between helping me and helping his friends, who are like family to him."

"I don't think that was a wise move, Avery."

"No kidding!"

"Is there any other way to avoid him having to choose?"

Avery had been thinking about that all morning. If she told Richard the truth, perhaps he would reconsider? If Richard understood how important this was to her, maybe they could find some sort of compromise? "Possibly." Or perhaps Richard would take one look and her at think it was a joke, and be more determined than ever to build his development. It was a gamble.

"You have to try. If you love him as much as you say, then you can't ask him to do this—not even for you."

As soon as the words were out of Jenna's mouth, Avery knew she was right. She'd thought of nothing else all morning. She supposed that was why she'd called Jenna—for confirmation of what she needed to do. It was just that last night Avery had been so overwhelmed by the depth of Quentin's feelings toward her, she hadn't thought about what this was costing him.

"I know you're right." Avery had to come clean and tell Richard of her existence. "I'm just not looking forward to what I have to do." After Leah's cold rejection of her, Avery was going to have to steel herself for what Richard might have in store. She was about to drop a bomb on him and she had to do it tonight.

"Well, whatever you need, I'm here for you."

"Thanks, Jenna. I might be taking you up on it later tonight."

On her way to the office, Avery dialed Richard King's phone number. His assistant told her that he was unavailable until after 5:00 p.m. "That's fine," she said, hanging up the phone. Now she just had to reach Quentin before he told Malik. The problem was when she called his cell, it went directly to voice mail, so she tried his home phone and still no answer. Where was he? He couldn't have just slipped off the face of the planet. She prayed she reached Quentin before he went to Dante's this evening.

"So, you've decided to heed my advice?" Jason asked Quentin when he delivered the photos of Richard King for *Capitalist* as promised later that afternoon.

"Yes, I have," Quentin replied, "but not for the reasons you think."

"So, the plot thickens." Jason regarded Quentin quizzically. He was surprised by Quentin's change of heart; his client was as stubborn as a mule. Jason was sure he was going to shoot himself in the foot. "So what changed your mind?"

"I'd rather not say. Just be satisfied to know that those photos are exactly what the magazine is looking for to promote King as a successful entrepreneur and businessman."

"All right," Jason said. "Keep your secret. I'm just happy to see that you aren't sabotaging the career you've worked so hard to achieve. So I guess our business is concluded for now. I'll touch base with you next week on that Samson Books deal."

"Thanks," Quentin said, rising from his chair and heading toward the door.

"Wait a sec," Jason said. "What about the photos of the center?"

"What difference does it make?" Quentin asked. "They'll never see the light of day, right?" He strode out the door without a backward glance. Now he had the unenviable task of facing his best friend for the second time and telling him he was reneging on his promise *again*. He felt like such a heel.

He pulled out his cell phone to check his messages and noticed he had four missed calls. All from Avery. He ignored them. He wasn't ready to talk to her right now. Afterward, he would, because she would be all he had left.

The King Corporation offices were very plush and swanky, Avery thought as she sat down in the waiting area Richard's receptionist had ushered her into. Although she was leaving for the day, she had assured Avery that everything was fine and that Richard would be out of his meeting momentarily.

His office door opened several minutes later and Richard emerged. "Avery." He came toward her and kissed her cheek. "I was so surprised, pleasantly so, when my receptionist said you requested a meeting with me today."

"Yes, well…" Avery was extremely nervous. She nodded at the associates as they departed. "It was a matter of extreme urgency and confidentiality."

"Well, come into my office," Richard said,

opening his arm so she could precede him. "Let's see how I can help."

Once he'd shut the door behind himself, Avery stood, not sure of how to begin. She watched him remove his suit coat and throw it over his chair. He was obviously very comfortable with her.

"Please have a seat." Richard gestured to the sofa across from his desk.

"Thank you," she said and sat on the edge. She fiddled by smoothing down her skirt. She was scared to death about revealing her true identity.

"What can I do for you?" Richard asked, taking a seat beside her. "Have you come to accept the position I offered?"

Avery shook her head. She wished it were that simple. "No, it's not that. You see, a couple of months ago, I learned some disturbing news about my past."

"Yes?"

"I learned that I was adopted."

"Adopted? Wow, that must come as quite a shock. You're…" Richard paused. "In your early thirties, right?" Avery nodded. "And you just learned this information?"

"Exactly."

"How can I help? Oh, wait, do you need some help finding your birth parents?" Richard lightly touched her cheek. "Well, my dear girl. My resources are at your disposal. I'll have my assistant put you into contact with the best private eye in the business."

Richard started to rise from the couch, but Avery halted him and he sat back down. She was acting strangely. Now he was really curious.

"I don't need one." She took a deep breath. She couldn't lose her nerve now. "I found my biological mother. She's remarried and living in Buffalo."

"That's great." He patted her knee. "You must be so relieved."

"I was, but it didn't turn out as I'd hoped." Avery swallowed.

"I'm sorry to hear that."

She wondered just how long he'd be this comforting once she told him the truth.

"Okay," Richard said, "so, if you're not here for my help, exactly why are you here, Avery?"

"Well…" She paused. If she didn't do this, Quentin would lose the only family he'd ever known and she couldn't ask him to go through that. She had to do this. "My biological mother's name is Leah Johnson, formerly Leah Gordon."

"Wh…who?" Richard stammered out the name.

"Leah Gordon," Avery continued. "I believe you know her?" She stared back into his green eyes.

Richard jumped up from the couch and walked over to the window. "I do," he said with his back to her, "but what does this have to do with me?"

Avery rose from the sofa and came to stand

behind Richard. "As you well know, you were involved with Leah nearly thirty-four years ago before you married Cindy." When Richard remained silent, Avery continued, "And the two of you had a love affair that resulted in a pregnancy."

Richard whirled around and faced Avery. "What are you saying?" he asked, even though he knew the answer.

"I'm saying that Leah gave up the baby for adoption."

"And?"

Avery paused for what seemed like an eternity before saying, "I am the result of that pregnancy." Once the words were finally out of her mouth, she felt liberated. No more secrets. The truth was out and now they had to live with the consequences. At least Quentin and his friends wouldn't be affected.

Avery waited for a response from Richard. She expected anger or for him to think she was lying. She was surprised when she got the exact opposite. Instead, he stared at her as if he was trying to memorize her features and match them to a woman he knew long ago.

"From the very first moment I saw you, I thought you reminded me of her," Richard said, "but never in my wildest fantasy would I have imagined this scenario." He rubbed his head as he stared back at Leah's same features and complexion.

"I don't understand this. She adamantly refused

to have an abortion because you were conceived in love. But if she believed that, how could she give you up?"

Avery was surprised at how torn he was by this information. "I guess you'd have to ask her that question yourself," she replied. Though she doubted Leah could give him very many answers; she sure hadn't given Avery much. "I never had any intention of telling you the truth, but unfortunately I need your help."

"What do you need? Whatever it is, I'll help you get it." Richard couldn't believe he was standing face-to-face with his daughter.

"I need you to back off the development deal you have in Harlem that would demolish the community center."

"What?" Richard was confused. "I don't understand, what does that deal have to do with you?"

"Quentin and his friends grew up in that center. His friend Malik Williams runs it and he's done a great job. You can't destroy it."

"And if I don't agree?" Richard asked. His eyes pierced hers. "You're going to go public with this information, aren't you?" Was his daughter really prepared to blackmail him? If so, she really was a chip off the old block.

"No, I'm not," Avery replied. "I'm asking you, Richard, to do the right thing. The community needs that center. It supplies free health and after-school care and many youth activities."

"I have a lot riding on this deal, Avery." Richard turned away and stared down at the rush-hour traffic fifty stories below.

"I realize that, but I'm asking you to do this for me," she pleaded. "This really means a lot to me and to the man I love."

"The man you love?" Richard asked, turning back to her. "I admit Quentin Davis is a decent fellow and I thought very highly of the young man, but you're in love with him?"

"Yes, I am. And that center meant everything to him growing up as an orphan. It still does. Without it, he would never have survived." Avery grasped his arm. "Richard, I am begging you, pleading with you, to please reconsider. For me," she added.

Richard didn't know what to say. He was standing in front of his and Leah's daughter. A daughter he never thought he'd have. He and Cindy had never been blessed with any children. After many miscarriages, they'd finally given up on having a child of their own. And Cindy had steadfastly refused adoption, so it had just been the two of them. And now his daughter, his flesh and blood was standing in front of him asking for his help. How could he possibly turn her down?

"All right, Avery." Richard didn't hesitate for a second. "I'll do it."

"Thank you." She reached over and hugged him tightly. She hadn't expected him to agree so easily. "You have no idea what this means to me."

"I've some idea," he said. "Or you would never have come forward. So what now?"

"What do you mean?"

"Can we have some type of relationship?" Richard asked. Now that he knew of her existence, he couldn't possibly turn his back on her.

Avery was surprised at the joy that shone in his eyes. She'd thought he'd want to sweep this under the rug. Keep her existence a secret. "Do you want one?"

"If you'll have me," he replied.

"I'd like that." She smiled and then glanced down at her watch. "Listen, I really have to get going." She had to catch Quentin before he said something he couldn't take back. "Thank you, Richard." She came forward, lightly pecked his cheek and rushed out of the room, leaving Richard staring after her, still holding his cheek.

"What's the big news?" Sage asked when Quentin came inside Dante's later that evening.

"Yeah," Malik concurred. "I love you guys and all, but two nights together? What's going on, man?"

"I have to talk to you about something and I know it's going to make you all unhappy so I thought I'd better tell you all at the same time," Quentin replied.

"Oh, no. This doesn't sound good at all," Dante commented, coming from behind the bar. He'd known Quentin was grappling with something the other day. And he guessed today was D-day.

"Does this have anything to do with some photos that you were going to send to *Capitalist*?" Malik asked.

"It does."

"So once again you're selling me out," Malik stated. "Once again the center loses out. I just don't understand it, Quentin. I thought I knew you, but apparently I was wrong."

"Quentin." Sage grasped his chin and forced him to look at her. But she couldn't read him. His face was clouded with uneasiness. "You wouldn't do this again. You wouldn't hurt Malik without cause, so why are you doing it now?"

"I can't tell you," Quentin said.

"Oh no you don't." Malik's face was a glowering mask of rage. "Don't back down like some coward. That's not the Q I know. So just tell us what the big darn secret is that's causing you to go back on your word *again*."

"I can't say. All I can tell you is this has to do with Avery."

"What does she have to do with why you can't help Malik?" Dante asked.

"I can't break Avery's confidence," Quentin said.

"Avery, Avery, Avery!" Malik yelled. "You know, Quentin, *Avery* was supposed to be a bet, a bet you seem to have forgotten. You were supposed to wow her with the Quentin Davis charm, get her into bed and move on. And now you're suddenly putting her over me. When did it change?"

"Malik, I—" But Quentin never got a chance to finish, because Sage nodded toward the doorway where Avery stood open-mouthed, staring back at him.

"Avery…" Quentin came toward her, but she put up a hand to stop him.

"Don't!" she replied as her face flushed crimson. "I just came to tell you that Richard is not going forward with his development deal."

"What do you mean?" Malik asked, taking a step toward Avery.

"I mean he is backing off. There will be no condos or multimedia complex," she informed the group.

"You're kidding!" Sage said. "How did you manage that?"

"He did it for me," Avery replied, looking directly at Quentin. "His daughter." And with that comment, she ran out the door.

Dante didn't understand. "Did she just say *his daughter?*"

"She sure did," Sage replied, slumping into a barstool with her mouth wide open.

"But I thought she was adopted?" Dante returned.

"She was," Quentin answered and took off after her.

"I guess that explains why she wouldn't want a

negative story on her biological father in the press," Sage said to Malik and Dante.

"And why Quentin refused to publish those photos," Dante added.

"Because he's in love with her," Malik finished. "And now I've just gone and ruined their relationship."

"It's not your fault," Sage replied, patting his back. "I just hope Quentin can fix this," she said, looking toward the door.

Chapter 15

Quentin ran down the street and caught up with Avery just as she was hailing a cab. "Avery, wait!" he shouted. In seconds, he'd bridged the gap between them. "Avery, please stop."

"Why should I?" She whirled around and faced him. Her eyes blazed with fury and her face was flushed with rage. It was almost enough to stop Quentin cold, but he persevered. "Clearly, I mean absolutely nothing to you."

The hurt he saw in those green depths tore right through to his very soul. "That's not true." He shook his head. Although he was ashamed at having taken advantage of her trusting nature when they'd begun dating, he loved her now more than words could say. He'd been prepared to give up everything for her.

"Isn't it?" Avery asked bitterly. She was furious at him. "I was nothing more than a bet to you, Quentin Davis. You used me for you and your friends' amusement. You guys must really have gotten a kick out of this." She was completely humiliated. Poor dumb Avery. They must have laughed and joked about her endlessly. She'd probably provided them with hours of entertainment.

Quentin met her accusing eyes without flinching. "I suppose initially it may have started out that way."

"You suppose? Oh, give me a break!" Avery scoffed as her lips thinned with anger.

"But things changed for me, Avery. The more I got to know you, the more I liked. You weren't some stuck-up rich girl, you were warm and funny and beautiful and amazing."

"And a sucker," she added just as a cab pulled up alongside the curb. "They say one is born every minute. And I guess today is my lucky day. Here I was thinking we had something special. I was way off the mark." She opened the taxi door.

Quentin halted her entrance. "Avery, you weren't off the mark. We do have something. Please give me a chance to make this up to you. To make things right."

"You can't, Quentin. You and I are through. History. Kaput." She slid inside the taxi and slammed the door. She rolled down the window and glowered at him. "Lose my number."

Quentin watched the taxi and the only woman he'd ever loved drive away into the night.

He returned to Dante's and found the crew assembled at the bar. "From your bereft expression, I take it things didn't go well?" Sage asked. Quentin's face was downturned and he looked in anguish.

"No, they did not." He took a seat beside her. He felt the changing tide. He'd seen the love fade in Avery right before his eyes and he'd been powerless to stop it.

"Just give her time," Sage said. "She's upset, hurt and probably embarrassed." She could only imagine how Avery felt. She'd have been just as upset if not worse.

"She thinks I don't care about her. That she meant nothing to me," Quentin replied. "Why didn't I tell her when I had the chance? All of this could have been avoided."

"Hindsight is twenty-twenty," Malik said.

"I thought you were angry with me." Quentin glanced sideways at him.

"I was, but when it all comes down to it, you're my brother, Q. And the last few weeks without all of you have been hell. So there, I said it. I missed you lugs."

Quentin smiled. At least something good had come out of this. They'd all realized just how important they were to each other. "And we missed you, didn't we?" Quentin glanced over at Sage and Dante.

"Yes," they said in unison.

"So, is this family drama finally over?" Sage asked. "Because I for one have had my fill of it."

"You and me both," Dante replied. He was tired of being the man in the middle.

"Now if only I could get Avery back," Quentin said wistfully.

"You can and you will," Sage said fervently. "I have never known you to give up on something without a fight and Avery Roberts will be no different. Go find that woman and make her yours."

"Mom, thank you so much for the use of the house in the Hamptons," Avery said the following morning when she stopped by her parents' home before getting on the road. When she'd called her mother last night, she'd been more than willing to part with the keys.

"It's no problem, sweetheart," her mother replied. "But can't you at least tell me what or *who* has upset you?"

"I don't really want to talk about it. All I want to do is get away for a while. You know, get some distance. And I hope some perspective." She was hoping to figure out where she'd gone wrong and how she could have let a man like Quentin dupe her so easily. She had some serious soul-searching to do.

"The Hamptons house is always a pleasant retreat," her mother said. "There's nothing more beautiful than walking along the shore collecting seashells or hearing the waves crash outside your window." It would be exactly what Avery needed. "Here's the keys." Veronica pulled the set out of her desk drawer.

"Thank you."

"How long will you be staying?"

"Oh, about a week or so." Hopefully, after she'd cried her eyes out, she could return to work and come back as the clear, levelheaded person she used to be. She didn't even recognize the spontaneous creature she'd become with Quentin Davis.

"Stay as long as you need," her mother said.

"I will. Thanks again, Mom." Avery squeezed her shoulders before leaving.

Quentin had tried to reach Avery several times over the last couple of days. He'd thought she was avoiding him until he'd finally broken down and called the gallery. That was when Hunter had informed him that Avery had taken a vacation. Where? He didn't know. The only person he could think of who would know where she was was her mother. And so he showed up on Veronica Roberts's doorstep midweek.

"Quentin, I'm surprised to see you," Veronica said when she opened the door.

"I'm sorry to stop by uninvited, Mrs. Roberts," Quentin apologized.

"You are always welcome, please come in," Veronica said and walked toward the living room. She thought very highly of him. "Please have a seat."

"Oh, I won't be staying long," Quentin said from the doorway.

"All right, well, what can I do for you?"

"I'm sure you've heard that Avery and I had a huge row."

Veronica chuckled. "Actually no, I hadn't. Avery was very closemouthed on this one. So you two had a fight? Well, that would explain her need for distance and perspective, as she called it."

"I made a huge mistake, Mrs. Roberts, and I fear Avery won't forgive me."

"Oh, pooh." Veronica threw her hand down. "Quentin, if she can forgive me, she most certainly can forgive you for whatever wrongs you've done. Just so long as you weren't unfaithful?" she asked.

"I was not unfaithful," Quentin replied. "But I was certainly less than forthcoming. And I want, no, I need to make this right, Mrs. Roberts. I love Avery."

"Of course you do." Veronica smiled. "I knew it the moment you came to get me after her biological mother rejected her. You knew exactly what to do to console her. You knew she needed me…. You bridged the gap between me and my daughter, and you have no idea how grateful I am for that, Quentin."

"It was my pleasure."

Veronica rose and walked over to her desk. "That's why I'm going to help you." She scribbled something on a piece of paper and handed it to Quentin.

"What's this?"

"It's the address and directions to our beach house in the Hamptons."

"Why?"

"It's where you will find my daughter and I hope bring her back to her senses. Because if she lets you slip through her fingers, it would be a great loss indeed."

"Thank you, Mrs. Roberts." Quentin bent down and brushed his lips quickly across her cheek.

"Oh!" Veronica smiled and touched her face. Quentin's eyes were sparkling with devilment. "You had better get out of here!"

"I will and when I come back I'll have Avery with me," he promised.

As Quentin took the two-hour ride to East Hampton, he recited over and over in his head the speech he wanted to give. He just hoped Avery would let him get the words all out. He didn't blame her for being angry with him. She had every right to be. He was no longer the cynical, commitment-shy man he'd been when he'd met her. In his previous relationship incarnations, he'd always been quick to leave and onto the next assignment. He'd never had the time for romantic entanglements, but Avery was different. With her, he'd opened up more than he had with any other woman. He'd told her what it was like growing up as an orphan. Sure, he'd known love from his grandmother. She'd reared him until he was ten and given him values, but when she passed, she'd taken his love right along with her. And he hadn't felt it since, at least not until Avery.

When Avery opened the door, she looked as beautiful as ever, barefoot, with her hair in a ponytail, wearing a bikini top and some skimpy shorts.

"What are you doing here, Quentin?" she said, folding her arms across her chest in an attempt to shield herself from Quentin's riveting male gaze. Even though she was angry with him, her breasts betrayed her by reacting to his nearness and growing taut.

"I came to make things right." He couldn't help but notice the steady rise and fall of her chest, even though she was furious with him.

"And how did you find me?" Avery asked despite knowing the answer to the question.

"A little birdie told me."

Her mother. Once again, the woman had a hard time minding her own business. "Well, she shouldn't have because I don't want to see you. Matter of fact, I don't want to have anything to do with you ever again in life." Avery tried to slam the door in his face, but Quentin managed to pry his foot in.

"Ouch, that's harsh," he said. "A lifetime is a long time." He tried to force his way in, but Avery pushed her whole weight against the door. "Are you sure you don't mean for a few weeks, perhaps a month?"

"Don't joke with me, Quentin. I am not in the mood. Why don't we just say the foreseeable future? Would that suffice?" When she couldn't hold the door any longer, Avery let go and ran to the back of the house. Before Quentin knew it, she was out the back door and headed to the stairs for the beach, but he followed her.

"Quite frankly, no, it wouldn't," he said from behind her. He had to jog to keep up with her. He didn't care that sand was getting in his shoes; he'd come to win Avery back and he wasn't leaving until he did.

"Running is not the answer, Avery," he said. "It's what I've been doing my entire life, but I'm not doing it anymore. That's why I'm here."

"Stay away, Quentin," she said over her shoulder as she walked along the beach. "Can't you see that I just want to be alone?"

When he didn't answer, she took off running down the shore. He caught up with her and grabbed her by the shoulders. His dark eyes bored into hers. "I am sorry, okay? I'm so sorry. I should have told you sooner. I was just afraid of losing you."

"*Sorry* doesn't cut it, Quentin." Avery tore herself out of his grasp. "You hurt me. After I gave myself to you so completely."

"I made a mistake. Can't you forgive me? Like you've forgiven your parents? Adoptive and biological? I know you have it within you, Avery. You have the capacity because you have a huge heart." He'd seen her forgiveness and compassion with her family. Why couldn't she do the same for him?

"You hurt me!" she yelled. "And now what, you're here to pick up the pieces? As if that were possible."

"It is if you allow it to be. If you give me another chance. Avery, I love you."

"Love? You don't know the meaning of the word," she said. "You're just saying it now to save face. So your friends will still think you're a great *playa.*"

"Avery, c'mon, think about it. If what you say is true, then why would I have been ready to trash my relationship with Malik if I didn't love you? I know you put yourself out on a limb for me by telling Richard, but I was willing to do the same for you. I was in essence ending a twenty-year friendship with the only family I've ever had. For you." Quentin titled her chin and forced her to look up at him. "For you, Avery. Because I love you."

"No, no, no." She shook her head and wrenched her arms out of his grasp. "You can't love me. Because I'm unlovable."

"Why would you say that?"

"My own mother didn't want me, why would I think you would? Mr. Smooth Operator. You're used to cutting and running. Why would I think you're in it for the long haul?"

"Because I never found a woman worth throwing in the towel for until now. When I met you, that changed. I finally stopped running away from love. Can't you see the difference? I feel it. After the childhood I endured, I didn't even think it was possible to fall in love with anyone, but I did. I fell in love with you, Avery, please believe that."

"My head is telling me to run in the other direction and not look back."

"And your heart?" Quentin asked, stroking her cheek. "What does it say?"

"My heart says to throw my arms around you and kiss you," Avery said. "But I don't know if I can trust you."

"You can, Avery. I promise you can," Quentin encouraged her. "You can trust me with your heart. And I promise I won't let you down again."

"I don't know." She shook her head.

"Baby, just do it. Just do what's in your heart."

Avery couldn't resist him any longer. She had to do what her heart craved. "I love you, Quentin

Davis!" She shouted and threw her arms around his neck. And when he wrapped his arms around her, lifting her off her feet, she knew she'd made the right decision.

"And I love you, Avery Roberts."

Much later, after they'd frolicked on the beach, splashing water on each other, they returned to the beach house where they made love slowly and languorously. There was a trail of strewn clothes across the beach house floor leading to the master bedroom.

Quentin's kisses that night were tender. His touch was sweet. Tears of happiness gleamed in Avery's eyes as his hands explored every inch of her feminine form, worshipping her.

"Thank you," Quentin said later.

"For what?"

"For giving me and us another chance. And for helping me escape the demons of the past. For showing me what true love is."

"You've done the same for me," Avery said, stroking his cheek. "I've made peace with the fact that I'm adopted and that I won't have a relationship with Leah. And that I could have one with Richard if I so desire. But if I don't, I have two wonderful parents who love me dearly. And I have you."

"We've both come a long way in a short time." Quentin ran his fingertips from her nose down across her sweet, sensual lips. "After that gallery opening, who would ever have thought we'd end up like this?"

"Oh, I had some idea." Avery smiled.

"You did not!"

"Well, maybe not in love, but from the moment I met you, I knew I wanted you."

"And you have me," Quentin said. "All of me. Any time you want."

The following weekend, Avery and Quentin joined the gang at Dante's for Sage's birthday party. At first Quentin wasn't sure about coming, given the fact that his friends had been in on the bet. He didn't want Avery to think any less of them, but she'd assured him that all was forgiven and that it was water under the bridge. She was a real trouper and walked in with a smile.

Sage was amazed at her courage. Avery had shown character and Sage could respect that. "I am so glad that you're here and that you forgave Quentin," Sage said, rushing toward Avery and giving her a hug. "It was stupid and childish and we should never have placed that bet. And I'm truly, truly sorry for my part in it."

But Avery interrupted her. "Let's leave that in the past, okay? And start fresh."

"You're very gracious. Thank you, Avery. And thank you for coming to my party." Sage couldn't believe she was thirty years old!

While Avery and Sage chatted, Quentin joined Malik and Dante at the bar.

"I didn't think you had it in you, my man," Dante said, coming forward and shaking Quentin's hand, "but you've found a great catch." He'd never seen Quentin look so happy, so fulfilled. From the huge grin on his face, the man was in heaven.

"I have," Quentin said, glancing at Avery. "And I don't intend to ever let her go."

"Don't you sound all possessive," Sage said as she and Avery came toward the men.

"Yeah, I'm a real he-man." Quentin pounded his chest.

Avery was surprised when Malik, of all people, said, "Welcome to the family, Avery," and gave her a warm hug. She would have thought he'd blame her for the trouble within their tight family unit. Apparently she was wrong, but then again that wouldn't be the first time. She'd misjudged Quentin when they'd first met.

"Thank you, Malik," she said when he released her. "We appreciate your support. Don't we, Quentin?"

When Avery looked up at him with those big green eyes and he saw the love that shone in them, Quentin was overwhelmed. He had everything he could ever want—a great career, great friends and an even better woman.

"Quentin?" Sage laughed. "Now that you're part of the family, Avery, you must call him Q."

"Oh? Well then, I love you, Q, Quentin Davis, with

all my heart and soul." She stood on her tiptoes and gave him a show-stopping kiss, which Quentin returned.

"And I love you, Avery Roberts."

ESSENCE **Bestselling Author**

DONNA
HILL

SEX AND LIES

Book 1 of the new T.L.C. miniseries

Their job hawking body products for Tender Loving Care
is a cover for their true identities as undercover operatives for
a covert organization. And when Savannah Fields investigates
a case of corporate espionage, the trail of corruption leads
right back to her husband!

Coming the first week of February wherever books are sold.

KIMANI™
ROMANCE

Mixing business with pleasure...

Acclaimed author

ANGIE DANIELS

the
PLAYBOY'S
PROPOSITION

Sheyna and her sexy boss, Jace, have a long history
of competition. Despite their mutual attraction, Sheyna
refuses to fall for the playboy. But when Jace wins a trip
with Sheyna at a bachelorette auction, the competition's
not over...until he loses his heart.

"Each new [Angie] Daniels romance is a true joy."
—*Romantic Times BOOKreviews*

Coming the first week of February wherever books are sold.

KIMANI™
ROMANCE

www.kimanipress.com

KPAD0530208

A dramatic new miniseries from

Bestselling author

DEBORAH FLETCHER MELLO

TO *Love* A STALLION

Book 1 of The Stallion Brothers

Marah Briscoe intends to use all her charm to keep ruthless CEO John Stallion from buying her family's ranch. Instead, she's blindsided by a man as infuriating as he is irresistible!

"Her description of scenes and characters is near perfect. The sassy dialogue…brings smiles."
—*Romantic Times BOOKreviews* on
Forever and a Day

Coming the first week of February wherever books are sold.

A Man Who Has Everything Needs...

More Than a Woman

National Bestselling Author

MARCIA KING-GAMBLE

Anais Cooper put her savvy and savings into creating a
charming day spa. The only problem is…her neighbor.
Former baseball star turned celebrity real estate mogul
Palmer Freeman has declared unofficial war on
her business venture. So she decides it's time to
add a little sugar to the mix!

Coming the first week of February
wherever books are sold.

ARABESQUE®

www.kimanipress.com

"*Eternally Yours*...A truly touching and heartfelt story that is guaranteed to melt the hardest of hearts."
—*Rendezvous*

USA TODAY Bestselling Author

BRENDA JACKSON

ETERNALLY YOURS

A Madaris Family Novel

Attorney Syneda Walter and fellow attorney Clayton Madaris are friends—and the last two people likely to end up as lovers. But things start to heat up during a Florida getaway and Clayton realizes Syneda is the woman for him. Can he help her heal old wounds and convince her that she will always be eternally his?

"Ms. Jackson has done it again!...another Madaris brother sweeps us off to fantasyland..."
—*Romantic Times BOOKreviews*

Coming the first week of February wherever books are sold.

ARABESQUE®

www.kimanipress.com

KPBJ0550208